DEMANDING
Discipline
LOVE AND CARE

SILVIA VIOLET

SEAN

"Kneel."

I glared at the very tall, very muscular, very confident man in front of me. "What if I don't want to?"

Blake raised a brow. I was naked. He'd commanded me to strip and I'd obeyed, thinking he would do the same, but he was still wearing his faded US Navy t-shirt and dark jeans. And a belt. A wide leather belt I knew would feel delicious on my ass, but I'd never tell him that. I wanted him to work for the privilege of spanking me.

"You do." He said it like he had no doubt. I got the feeling he didn't have doubts about much.

I turned and walked across his bedroom, tightening the muscles in my ass to give him the best view.

"Sean, I told you to kneel, and I mean for you to do it now."

I wanted to. I wanted to be at his feet, but I couldn't just give in. That would mean… I wasn't sure exactly what, but it wasn't who I was. I didn't take orders. I loved to be spanked, to be fucked hard and held down, but I didn't actually want to be a man's submissive. So many Doms I'd met took everything way too seriously anyway. I liked sex, and I liked games. That's all this was, a game. Except Blake didn't seem to agree.

"And if I don't?" I asked.

"You will." He remained just as confident as he'd been since he'd approached me at Thrust.

Worse. He was right. The bastard. No way was I going to give up the chance to have whatever he wanted to give me. I'd had my eye on Blake ever since a friend mentioned seeing him do a pony play demo at Thrust. I'd stumbled across some pony play porn a few months ago, and wow. I had no idea how hot a guy could be with a tail plug up his ass. I'd ordered one for myself and played around with it, but it wasn't the same without a partner.

I walked around the room, glanced out the window, and finally came to stand by Blake again. I reached out, intending to touch his cock, hoping that would break his intense concentration. His fingers clamped around my wrist, and he squeezed tightly enough to let me know that if he didn't want me to touch him, I wasn't going to be able to.

Blake looked at the floor, making clear what he still wanted. I sank to my knees without further protest. Blake had this presence that made me want to obey. I wanted to hate him for it, but I didn't.

"Better," he said, his voice cool and even.

I looked up at him. "It might be, but I still don't know what you're going to do to me now that you have me here. Are you going to make me be your pony? I heard you like that."

He tilted his head and studied me. He was silent for so long I thought he wasn't going to answer, but then he said, "Do you like pony play?"

"I... um... I like tail plugs."

He gave the barest hint of a smile. "You might like pony

play for the accessories, but what you need it for is the discipline."

I bristled at this, no matter how true it was.

"Pony play can be about a lot of different things," Blake said. "I had a partner who was seriously into it, and we went to events together. I no longer do that, but I would consider letting you be my ponyboy to help you learn how to obey my commands."

No. No way. I didn't need obedience training. I wasn't a dog—or a wild pony. "That's not... I don't..."

"We can talk about that later."

"So if you aren't going to make me wear a tail, what are you going to do?"

"I'm not going to make you do anything. I'm going to ask, and you're going to either choose to obey or use your safeword."

I'd told him my safeword—licorice—and I trusted he would stop if I used it. Alan, the owner of Thrust, had hired Blake as a security consultant, and Alan would never do business with someone who didn't treat subs well.

The problem was, I didn't want Blake to stop. I hoped he was going to ask me to swallow his cock. I hadn't seen it yet, but based on the bulge in his jeans, it was enormous, and I wanted to feel it in my mouth.

Blake seemed to be waiting for me. To safeword? To challenge him? I wasn't sure. Finally he broke the silence. "Keep your gaze down, and don't speak unless I ask you a question. My safeword is red. If I use it, you're no longer expected to follow my rules, and if you're restrained, I'll release you immediately."

"Wait. You're the Dom. Why do you need a safeword?"

"A situation can make a person uncomfortable no matter how much control they believe they have."

I supposed that made sense. I looked down like he'd told

me to. Not because I was really submitting, but because I wanted to know what he'd do next. Sooner or later his cock would be mine.

Instead of unzipping his pants like I'd hoped, Blake walked over to the bed and sat down. I could just see him out of the corner of my eye. His hands went to his belt, and he unfastened it slowly. I turned my head a tiny bit to see better.

"Eyes down."

Shit. He hadn't even been looking at me. How had he known I'd moved? Fucking Navy SEAL magic, most likely.

At least if I put up with his high-handed demands, I'd be able to say I'd fucked a SEAL. That had been on my bucket list since I was like thirteen.

I heard a whoosh that had to be him pulling the belt through its loops. I jumped when he cracked it against his leg. *Fuck.* That sound shouldn't be so hot.

"Come over here and kneel by me."

I started to stand.

"No. Hands and knees only."

He wanted me to fucking crawl. "I don't—"

"I didn't ask you to speak, Sean. Use your safeword, or do what I said."

I did what he said. It was fucking embarrassing, and my cock loved it.

"Satisfied?" I asked when I was next to him.

"No."

"But I—"

"You did what I said, but what I really want is for you to admit you enjoyed it."

"I told you. I like to be spanked. I like for a man to dominate me in bed, but I'm not really a submissive."

"I know what you said."

"Then why—"

He laid his finger against my lips, stopping me from

saying more. I looked down at his belt. He'd made a loop with it and was holding it up as if taunting me with it. He raised his hand and caressed my cheek with the cool leather.

"I want to spank you with this. May I do that, boy?"

I nodded, resenting how much I liked him calling me boy. From anyone else, I would hate it. I wasn't a kid. I was a man. A man who liked sex and belts and spanking and—

"I need to hear your answer."

"Yes, sir."

The "sir" slipped out against my will. Something about Blake made me incapable of holding it back.

"Lay over my lap and present your ass to me."

I shook my head. I'd been spanked while I was bent over a bed, on my hands and knees, and on a spanking bench, but the idea of lying over his lap was much more humiliating. It made me feel like I deserved to be punished rather than given pleasure.

"Now, Sean."

My heart pounded, the sound loud in my ears. Could I do this? Did I want to? I could use my safeword, and end this, but… I looked at his belt again, then stretched my naked self over his lap. His worn jeans felt soft against my chest and stomach. I let my head hang down, and braced myself on the floor.

Blake laid an arm over my waist and gripped me firmly. "Shout, beg, or cry all you want, but try to stay still. I don't want to hurt you."

"Isn't the belt going to hurt?" Wasn't that the point?

He chuckled. "Yes, but I meant really hurt you, damage you, instead of just reddening your ass."

I started to say something, but he hit me with the belt before I could. The blow wasn't hard. It stung though, and I started to wonder if I'd gotten in over my head.

"I'm going to start slow," Blake said. "Do you know what to do to make me stop?"

"Say my safeword."

"Remind me what it is."

"Licorice." I hated the stuff, so it had seemed a good choice.

"Take a deep breath."

I did, no longer even wanting to resist. How had he pushed past my barriers so fast?

"Now exhale."

When I did, he slapped my ass and pain exploded across my skin. "That's starting slow?"

He didn't respond. He also didn't spank me again. Seconds passed. I squirmed against his hold, both wanting more and wanting to be free.

Crack. He brought the belt down across the other ass cheek. Now they both throbbed.

Two more blows. One after the other.

Blake didn't say anything, and I wasn't sure if words would've helped or made things worse.

The strokes started to come faster, and I struggled to breathe. "Too much. It's too much."

He didn't slow down. I strained against his hold and made embarrassing whimpering sounds. The blows from his belt hurt more than any spanking I'd had, but I didn't want him to stop. My cock had softened at first, but it was hard again now, hard and desperate for friction.

"Don't you dare come," Blake said as if he'd read my mind.

I didn't know if I could hold back, but he slapped me harder, and I cried out, forgetting everything but the pain.

"I'm going to give you five more like that. And you're going to count them."

"No!" I fought his hold. I needed to get away, needed to—

"Sean, do you remember how to make me stop?"

"Want this," I squeaked.

"You want me to keep going?"

"Yes, you fucking bastard. Yes."

"One extra for that." He cracked the belt across my ass, and I cried out, sounding so lost.

"Please."

"Count. I'll make you repeat every one you miss."

I whimpered. "Hurts too much."

He caressed my back, running his hand up and down my spine. "I know it hurts, but this is what you need. Do you trust me?"

"Yes." The word came out as a sob. Tears spilled over, rolling down my cheeks. It was humiliating for him to be able to break me down like this. I'd never cried during a spanking. I knew some people used them as a release, but it had always just been foreplay to me.

"I'm starting now," he said, his voice calm and steady.

Crack. I whimpered, but I felt disconnected from everything, like if I just let go I could float away from the pain.

"Sean?"

Count. Have to count. "One." My voice was rough and barely audible, but Blake must have been satisfied, because he brought the belt down again.

I jerked in his arms, trying to escape pain even as I arched my back, reaching my ass out for more. My cock was still rock hard. "T-two."

"That's right. You're doing so good." His praise seemed to lessen the fire burning across my ass.

Crack!

"Three." The word came out strangled as I shuddered from the pain.

"Good, Sean. Such a good boy. Just two more, and we'll be done."

"Four," I shouted when the next blow came. Tears chased

one another down my cheeks. I was happy and sad at the same time, hurting but feeling so good. My whole body felt lit up and I needed this to end, needed to come, needed Blake.

The last blow was the hardest of all, and I cried out, writhing as if I could escape the sting.

"I'm waiting," Blake said.

I tried to find my voice, but all I could do was whine.

He slapped my ass with his hand. The blow wasn't hard, but it still hurt like hell.

"F-five."

He dropped the belt and bent to kiss my neck as he rubbed my stiff shoulders. "I'm so proud of you, Sean. I knew you could do this."

Proud? He was proud of me? Instead of stopping the tears, that just made them fall faster.

"Thank me, Sean, for giving you what you needed."

"Thank you, sir." The words were out before I could stop them.

"Good boy." He ran his hand through my hair, petting me. Then he helped me onto the bed. I was sitting on my ass, but the painful throb seemed far away.

Blake knelt between my legs and pulled me to him for a kiss. His lips were soft and warm against mine, and he was tender with me, so different from the serious, merciless man who'd struck my ass. In a way, though, that gentle kiss hurt more than the spanking, because it made me long for things I couldn't have. I wasn't going to allow myself to be vulnerable. I knew where that could lead, and no way in hell was I going there. I groaned as he teased my lips, opening them with his tongue then pushing into my mouth the way I wished he'd thrust into my ass.

As frightened as I was by the intensity of what I felt for him, I couldn't make myself pull away. I wrapped my arms around his neck and slid my fingers into his short hair. It was soft and silky, so unlike the rest of him. I massaged his scalp, and he growled against me, the kiss growing more aggressive.

When he finally pulled back, we were both short of breath. He stared at me, and I couldn't look away. I knew he saw too much of what I wanted to hide. I loved what he'd done, loved having him take charge, no matter how much I resisted.

"I'm going to fuck you now." Blake's voice was low and gravelly, and my cock liked that a lot. "You're going to get on your hands and knees at the end of the bed and offer your ass to me. You will not come until I say you can. Is that clear?"

I looked into his gray-green eyes and tried to force some air into my lungs.

"Sean?"

"Yes, sir." The words spilled so easily from my lips.

He smiled, and I positioned myself for him, wishing I knew how to truly surrender, to make this easier so there wasn't part of me that was always fighting.

"Such a good boy." I shuddered when he rubbed my sore ass, pleased he could see something in me that I couldn't see in myself.

"That hurts."

"Of course it does. But it feels good too, doesn't it?" His voice was calm, so measured. I wondered if I could make him lose control. Did he ever feel conflicted like I did? Probably not. He was like a solid wall of dominance, warm but unyielding.

And I fucking loved it, even as part of me wanted the kind of fast, wild fuck I usually got, the kind I walked away from as soon as we'd both come. When sex was really good, I'd jerk off to the memory of it, after I was home, savoring that second orgasm, then falling asleep in my own bed, pretending to be satisfied.

"You're thinking too much," Blake said.

"That's not something I get accused of often."

He slapped my ass, and I gave a startled cry. "Any more sass from you, and I won't allow you to come. Do you understand me, boy?"

"If I'm your boy, do you expect me to call you Daddy... sir?" I tacked the last bit on, thinking maybe I'd get away with the question that way.

He leaned over me until his mouth was right by my ear. "Do you want to call me Daddy?"

"No, that's weird and... No." I didn't, did I? I'd always thought that was a little too wrong, but then why did my dick jump when I said it?

He chuckled. "That didn't sound very convincing. You need a Daddy, that's for sure. I can be that for you, or you can call me sir, but you will show me respect."

The part of me that had no sense of self-preservation wanted to mouth off again, to see if I could make him lose his cool, but my cock was so hard it hurt. I would do almost anything to get relief, so I just said, "Yes, sir. I'll be good."

"Head down on the bed and hold yourself open for me."

My ass was hot under my touch and tugging on the sore skin hurt enough to make me whimper, but I did as he said, showing him my hole.

"That's good, boy. Stay just like that. I've got to get the lube and a condom."

"Thank you, sir." Whoa. Where had that come from? Why was I thanking him for making me expose myself like an eager slut? The fact that I was an eager slut was obviously beside the point.

He must have used the lube on his way back, because the second he reached me, he slid a slick finger along my crack, making me shiver. "You're so hot like that, boy, all open and ready. Tell me what you want."

I was used to telling my sex partners exactly what I wanted and expecting them to give me precisely that. Sometimes my demands got me spanked or held down or tied up, but they always ultimately got me what I wanted. With Blake, though, it was different. He wanted me to admit how much he affected me, and I wasn't sure if he'd give me what I asked for, even if I begged. And with him, what I wanted was so much more than I'd ever wanted from anyone else. I wanted to be broken, stripped down to nothing, owned. I pressed my lips together to keep from spilling out all my secrets.

"If you don't talk, I'll assume you're satisfied and just jerk myself off."

"No!" I couldn't let him leave me like this.

"So you do want something?"

"Smug bastard," I muttered.

"What was that?"

"Nothing."

"What did you say, Sean?"

"I said you're a smug bastard."

"You're right. I am." He reached under me and took my cock in his hand, which was not what I'd been expecting. He gripped me firmly as he slid his hand up and down. In seconds, I was panting so hard I was dizzy. I worked my hips, pushing into his fist. I was close, so fucking close. I wouldn't be able to hold back if he kept this up.

"Please. I'm going to come."

"No, you're not."

"Blake, please. I really can't."

He ignored me and kept going. My balls were so tight. I was right there. Sweat dripped down my neck as I fought what seemed inevitable.

Then he let go and stepped away from me. My cock

pulsed, almost like I was coming without actually shooting my load. I'd never been that close and stopped before. It fucking hurt.

"Let's try this again," Blake said, voice still completely even. "Tell me what you want."

I was too out of breath to speak at first, but finally, I said, "I want your cock in me. I want you to fill my ass, to fuck me hard, to make me beg."

"See, that wasn't so hard."

Fuck you. "Yes, sir."

"Don't move until I tell you otherwise."

I already felt like I was going to come out of my skin. Even without him touching me, I was fighting not to fuck the air. How was I going to obey him?

He pressed a thick finger into me. It felt good, but it wasn't nearly enough.

"More," I gasped.

"You'll get more. But you have to be patient."

"Not good at that."

"I could teach you to be."

I whimpered, but I kept myself from telling him how much I wanted that.

"I love the sounds you make. So desperate."

He added a second finger, and I pushed back, trying to take them deeper.

"Stay still," he commanded.

"I can't. Please, I—"

"No more talking."

"But you said?"

He slapped my ass, and I bit back a sob. Why was I letting him do this? I couldn't talk. I couldn't move. What was I supposed to do?

"Just feel."

Fuck. Was he reading my mind now?

He added another finger and pushed deeper, dragging the digits over my prostate. I shook with tension as I fought to stay still. He slid his fingers out and back in, and I couldn't help but flex my hips. I needed this, needed to be fucked.

"I can tell you're trying to obey. You want to be good, you just need more training."

I didn't want to be trained; I wanted to be fucked. Somehow I managed to keep those words inside, even though I wanted to shout them. I had no doubt Blake would deny me the chance to come if I kept fighting him.

I was rewarded for my good behavior by the tip of his cock teasing my hole. And then finally, he pushed into me slowly, so fucking slowly.

2

BLAKE

I squeezed Sean's ass just to hear him hiss. The way he writhed under me was fucking incredible. I loved that he seemed to finally be surrendering to what he needed from me.

The first time I saw him, he was playing with someone at Thrust. He'd taunted the Dom, and the man had spanked him harder, but Sean had never dropped his bratty act, never really given in. I'd decided right then that I wanted to see if I could earn his submission. I needed a challenge. I'd been out of the Navy for two years now, and while I liked my job as a security consultant, I was restless and itching to do something meaningful. Taking care of Sean's needs would be perfect.

Right now what he needed was to come so hard, he'd be forced to admit how good things could be between us. Having had a taste of him, I was even more determined to make him mine.

"You ready for my cock, boy?"

"Yes, dammit! I've been ready."

I wasn't going to let him get away with being a brat. "No, I don't think you are. Not with that attitude."

"Fuck. I'm sorry, sir."

I held myself still, wanting to see what he'd do.

"Please, sir. I want your cock."

"Much better, boy." I surged forward, pushing past the tight ring of muscle that wanted to keep me out.

"God, yes. That's what I need," Sean shouted, but he whined as I sank deeper into him, sounding so very needy.

"I'm going to fill you so full you won't be able to think about anything but my cock."

"I already can't."

"Good." I pulled back and thrust harder, sinking all the way in.

He gasped. "So full."

I was going to come much too fast if he kept talking like that. "Your ass is squeezing me so tight. I love how it feels to be inside you."

He whimpered and pushed back against me. "Please fuck me, sir."

"Since you asked nicely, you'll get what you want, but you're still not allowed to move."

I pulled out and drove back in, making him cry out. I didn't stop that time, but I kept my strokes slow, wanting to torment him. I couldn't take it for long, though. A few moments later, I increased the pace until I was driving into him hard enough to push him toward the headboard.

"Brace yourself; I'm not going to show your ass any mercy."

He murmured something, likely calling me a bastard again, but I let it go. I could always punish him later. Right now I didn't want to do anything but own his ass.

"Arch your back." He did, and my next thrust made him cry out.

"Fuck, yes! Please. Right there."

"Is that what you need?"

"Yes, Daddy, yes."

Holy shit. I hadn't expected him to call me that, and it brought me right to the edge. This wasn't going to last much longer. I gripped his hips and fucked him even harder, making sure I kept the angle just right.

"Need to come. Please," he begged as he tried to reach under himself. I grabbed his wrist and pinned it to the mattress.

"You'll come when I allow it."

"Please! Can't wait."

"Yes, you can." If I had my way, I'd prove Sean could do a lot of things he didn't think he could now. I imagined him on all fours with a tail plug in his ass, bridle straps across his cheek, and a bit in his mouth. Fuck, that would be hot. And it would be perfect for teaching Sean how to obey.

He was panting and working his hips, trying to meet every one of my thrusts despite my hold on him. I knew I was pushing him hard, so I decided to change tactics. "Now it's my turn not to move. Fuck yourself on my cock, but do not come."

"Y-yes, sir."

When I let go of his hips, it was all I could do to keep him from knocking me backward. He was wild, driving back against me without any rhythm at all. I doubted he could hold on much longer, so I took pity on him and reached for his cock.

"You've done so good, boy. I want you to come for me now, show me how much you love my cock."

Sean fucked me even harder then. "I love it so much. Please, sir."

I wrapped my hand around his shaft and worked him as

fast and hard as he rode me. In seconds, he spurted over my hand and onto the bed.

I'd meant to hold myself back, but between his ass squeezing my cock and the sounds he made, I couldn't take any more denial so I let go and fucked him in rough jabs as I filled the condom.

When we were both wrung dry, we collapsed onto the bed. I rolled to my side to keep from crushing him, and he surprised me by turning to look at me. "That was..." He licked his lips and tried again. "That was amazing."

I smiled. "It was, and I want to do that again."

"Give me a few minutes, Mr. Navy-SEALs-Need-No-Recovery-Time."

Damn, I loved his snark. "I didn't mean now or even tonight. I meant I want to see you again."

Sean frowned. "I don't really... I don't think—"

"Did you enjoy this?"

He was studying the ceiling now, but after a few seconds, he nodded.

"There's a lot more we can enjoy together, including a tail plug and a bridle."

He made a strangled sound, but he shook his head. "You want me to submit to you, to really submit, to like it?"

"I do."

"You want to train me?"

"You need discipline, Sean. In fact, I think you crave it. I want to give that to you. I want to take care of you."

"I'm not a child. When I called you Daddy, I didn't mean it. I don't know what made me do that."

"I almost came when you said it."

He turned to me then, eyes wide. "Seriously?"

"Yes."

His cheeks pinkened, and he looked down. "It feels so wrong."

17

"Good wrong or bad wrong?"

"Umm… Bad wrong which feels good?"

I laughed. "I can work with that."

He gave a small smile. "I'm not what you want."

He sounded so sad, and it made my chest ache.

I brushed his hair off his forehead and cupped his face in my hands. "I think you're wrong."

"I'm not really submissive. I just like impact play."

"Are you sure about that?"

He took a shaky breath. "I thought I was."

That was a more honest answer than I expected. "Do you feel differently after tonight?"

"You forced me to do things I didn't think I'd like, but I… Fuck, I just wanted more."

His words made me uneasy. I needed to make sure he had truly wanted what we'd done, that he wasn't just too stubborn to stop me. "Did I force you? Really?"

"You didn't give me any options except my safeword."

"You do know that's a legitimate option, right? I don't want to push past any serious limits."

"I wanted all of it."

His voice was so soft I barely heard him.

"Say that again."

"You heard me. Don't SEALs have supersonic hearing?" He stuck his lip out in an adorable pout that likely won him exactly what he wanted from most men.

"No, but we have a heightened awareness of our surroundings, so I see most things too."

He huffed, but I was glad of the reassurance he'd wanted everything we'd done.

"I think you're exactly what I want."

"And what is that?" Sean asked.

"A challenge."

He laughed, but it sounded bitter. "Avery would say you're right there."

"I can give you what you need too."

"How can you know what I need? I don't even know myself, and any time I think maybe I do, it turns out I'm wrong."

I took his hand in mine and squeezed it. "I think you need patience and discipline, but to get there, I think you need to learn to let go."

"And your belt can help me with that?"

"Did it tonight?"

He glared at me. "Fuck, yes."

I wanted to push him to say yes right now, but I knew that wasn't right. He needed to be totally into this or it wouldn't work. I'd end up scaring him off. "Think about it, okay, and if you want more, you know where to find me."

Sean rolled onto his back again and sighed. "I do, but can you be the one to contact me?"

"Sure, but I won't know when you're ready, or if you're ready."

"Even if I am, I won't call. I never follow through. I'll just keep running from you, from this, from having any fucking discipline." The desperation in his tone made me ache.

"Sean, look at me."

It took him a few seconds, but he did. "I'm going to text you in three days, but you have to promise me something."

"What?"

I chose to ignore his snappy tone. We'd work on that. "Promise that if you truly don't want what I'm offering, you'll say no."

He nodded. "Trust me, I won't agree if I don't want to. I never see guys twice unless we have like a fuck buddy understanding or something. It's not worth getting hurt or hurting someone else."

"I'm not going to hurt you. I will push your boundaries though."

He nodded. "I can't promise not to push back."

"That's what spankings and other punishments are for."

"What if I want to be spanked?"

"Sometimes what we want and what we need are the same thing, and that's beautiful. But if we're going to try this, you're going to have to trust me to know what you need."

"I… Shit. Avery's going to laugh so hard."

I frowned. "Why?"

"He's been saying I need someone to take me in hand forever, and I just laughed and told him he needed to stop trying to involve me in his kinky shit."

"You're a regular at Thrust. Doesn't that make you pretty kinky already?"

"I never do anything but a little spanking and light bondage. I go there with Avery because it feels illicit, and Doms tend to like my ass."

I raised my brows, and he laughed. "Well, they do."

"It is a nice ass."

"Damn right."

He sat up and ran a hand through his hair, which was hopelessly disarrayed. The gel he'd used was now making it stick straight up. But he seemed to have gotten his equilibrium—and his sass—back.

He stretched and exhaled loudly. "I should go."

"You don't have to. I could make you a snack or—"

"Thanks, but I'm fine. I just… I'm not used to talking after sex."

I wanted to order him to stay, but we weren't there yet. I needed to let him have some space to process what we'd done.

As he got dressed, he was practically vibrating. He looked everywhere but at me. I got up to walk him to the door.

"Are you sure you're all right to drive?"

He frowned. "I didn't drink anything."

"I know, but you seem shaky."

I could tell he didn't like that I'd noticed. "I'm fine. I really am, okay? I'm just... tired."

He was clearly lying, and I was sure he knew I wasn't fooled. But he was a grown up, and I wasn't his keeper, not yet anyway.

"All right. Just be careful."

"Yes, Daddy." His tone dripped with sarcasm.

I grabbed his arm. "Don't say that if you don't mean it."

He sucked in his breath. "I don't know what I mean right now."

"You've got a few days to figure it out."

I watched him walk away. His ass looked damn fine in his tight jeans, and I was sure he knew it. I hoped he would agree to see me again, because I hadn't had an evening this good in... ever.

3

SEAN

I STARED at Blake's text. He wanted to know if we could see each other again on Saturday. Shit, why had I told him to contact me?

You would've seen him again at Thrust anyway.

Or I could just never go there again.

And where else would you go to find a man to redden your ass?

Maybe I should just move. I want a change anyway.

You've got to stop running every time you get the least bit bored.

Sometimes I hated my conscience. I didn't run from things, not really. I made a decision to leave if something wasn't what I thought it should be. Why waste time on things I hated? Not that I hated being with Blake. I fucking loved it. The way he told me what to do in that voice that made clear he would not be contradicted. No other man had actually made me want to surrender.

I glanced at the bowl of Cocoa Puffs I'd been scarfing down for dinner. Maybe I did need someone to spank me into shape. Or crop me. While I wore a tail.

Fuck. I'd known from the moment I agreed to go home with Blake that I wasn't going to be able to walk away like I usually did. Normally, if I were even thinking about round two with a man, I'd make him wait, ignore his texts until he tried again or I got too horny. I wanted Blake, but I didn't have to let him know how much, did I?

Why don't you try acting like a fucking adult for a change?

I thought about the night Blake and I had spent together. The way he'd forced me to kneel, made me bend over his lap, made me thank him. The vivid memories had my cock thickening.

I glanced back down at the phone.

What was I going to do? I didn't want to start a relationship. But it wouldn't really be dating if I just let him spank me and order me around and maybe dress me up like a pony, right? There didn't have to be feelings involved. There couldn't be. I'd sworn not to give my heart to anyone. Not after what my mom had gone through. I didn't force myself to do anything that didn't make me happy, and I wouldn't let someone hurt me emotionally. Beating my ass was okay, though. I could let Blake do that again. I'd just have to be clear about my boundaries.

Saturday works for me.

I have a private room for us at Thrust. Be there at 8.

He'd booked a room before he asked me? What if I'd said no? I started typing out an angry text, but I erased it, proving I could be an adult when I wanted to.

Maybe he had a standing reservation. Alan was a client, so he could probably get a room whenever he wanted. Would he have found someone else to fuck there if I hadn't shown up? I didn't like thinking about that.

What if I'd rather come at 9?

Then I'll be even more convinced you need discipline.

I hated how much that turned me on. How far could I push him?

What if I like being undisciplined?

This isn't about what you like; it's about what you need.

I unzipped my jeans and took out my cock, which was fully hard now.

How do you know what I need?

I stroked faster as I watched the little dots roll across the screen, telling me he was responding.

The lock started to turn in the door, and I jumped. I tried to run for my room, but I slipped on a shirt I'd dropped there while second-guessing my outfit that morning. I slid a few feet and then lost my balance entirely and ended up in a heap on the floor.

"Sean?" Avery, my roommate, was clearly trying to hold back a laugh. "What the hell are you doing?"

"I... uh..." I tried to push myself to my feet, more concerned about my phone, which had fallen from my hand. It was only after I grabbed it and assured myself the screen wasn't cracked that I remembered my dick was hanging out.

"For fuck's sake, Sean. Were you just standing there jerking off?"

"Yeah. So what? You weren't home."

Avery made an exasperated sound. "You knew I would be home any minute, and I could've had Felicity with me, or worse, Felicity *and* Carter."

I shrugged. "Carter needs to lighten up, especially if he's going to be married to her."

"Lightening up does not include seeing your fiancé's best friend's roommate's dick."

"Whatever." My phone vibrated, and I glanced down at it.

I know exactly what you need, because I felt you shiver while I spanked you, felt you surrender to me as you let yourself enjoy it. I saw how you loved being on your knees.

You're wrong.

He sent a raised brow emoji.

Fine. 8:00 on Saturday.

Be on time.

"Are you seriously not even going to zip your pants or go in your room?" Avery asked as he made himself a Cape Cod.

"I'll zip up if you make me one of those too."

He grabbed another glass, and I set the phone down and tucked myself back in.

"Who were you texting?" he asked after we'd both taken a few sips.

"No one."

"So you were just frowning at your phone and typing for no reason? With your dick out, I'll add."

"You've seen my dick a million times."

Avery rolled his eyes. "That is so not the point."

"It was just some guy." I took another sip, trying to look nonchalant.

"Some guy you're about to hook up with?"

"Some guy I did hook up with."

Avery's eyes went wide. "You gave him your number?"

Shit, why did I say that? "I was drunk."

"You don't go home with guys when you're drunk, not after…"

He was right. After waking up bound to a guy's bed with two guys I didn't recognize passed out beside me, I swore off combining drinking and hooking up. It was one or the other for me.

"Sean, what are you holding back? Who is this guy?"

"Nobody important."

Avery scowled at me. "You wouldn't have responded to his text or been about to jerk off while texting him if he wasn't important."

"Fine." Avery wasn't afraid to keep poking at me until he wore me down. I might as well get it over with. "He's someone I know from Thrust, and Saturday night we hooked up."

"How well do you know him?"

"Alan approves of him. He's totally safe. Too safe, really."

Avery smiled as he drank from his Cape Cod. "Someone who expects you to play by the rules?"

"I use rules. I have a safeword."

"No, I mean someone who wants you to really surrender."

Heat filled my face. How did Avery know? "I like to be spanked. That's it. I've told you that a million times."

"Uh huh."

I flipped him off.

Avery started scrolling through his phone. "What should we get for dinner?"

Thank God he wasn't going to push me more. "Sparky's."

Avery pondered my suggestion for a moment. "I shouldn't."

"Yes, you should."

"Why?"

"Because I want it, and no one should say no to spicy fried chicken or fries or banana pudding."

Avery groaned.

"You know you want it."

"Fine. But you have to go get beer. We're out."

I gave him my best pouty face. "Can't we have that delivered too?"

"There's a shop on our block. I'm not paying extra for delivery."

"Fine. You know what I want, right?"

"Yeah. Better than you, apparently."

"Fuck off."

Avery flipped his hair off his face. "Not tonight. I'm much too tired."

"Order my damn food."

"Yes, sir." He smirked.

I grabbed my keys and wallet and started for the door.

"You should probably fasten your pants before you go out."

I looked down. While my cock was back in my briefs, my pants were gaping open. "If you insist."

"I don't, but people on the street likely will."

I sighed as I pulled up the zipper. "Am I really that big of a mess?"

"Sometimes. But I love you."

"Love you too." And I did. Avery was the best roommate ever. I loved him so much I might even buy his favorite beer; at least, if they didn't have mine.

I was twenty minutes late for our second date. It wasn't really my fault. Avery came with me to Thrust, and a few guys he knew came up to us. I didn't want to be rude, so I started talking to them. Maybe I was feeling a little nervous and second-guessing whether I should meet Blake at all, and maybe it was Avery who realized what time it was and pushed me—literally—toward the private rooms, so I wouldn't ditch Blake.

Blake wasn't visibly angry. He was infuriatingly calm and controlled just like he'd been the week before. He punished me for being late, using a wicked leather-covered paddle. Then he made me kneel on the hard floor and watch him jerk off until he came all over his hand. I was sent home with my dick aching and orders not to come. Fuck that. I jerked off the second I got in the house.

I ignored Blake the first time he called me after that, but I couldn't stop thinking about being his ponyboy. I was late to get my hair cut by Avery the next day, because I was watching pony play porn and obsessing about how it would feel to have a tail swishing against the back of my legs while I sucked Blake off.

Eventually, my resolve gave, and I agreed to another date with Blake, and then another after that. I actually got to come during both of those evenings, though Blake made me wait ages for it. He liked driving me to the brink of insanity before letting me come while forcing me to acknowledge that I wanted what he demanded, no matter how humiliating it was.

He finally put a bridle on me and made me prance around his apartment. I felt ridiculous, but I wanted his cock in me so I did it. In fact, I did everything he asked with only minimal resistance. Well, I thought it was minimal. But he wasn't satisfied and he expected me to earn privileges like tasting his cock or wearing a tail. I couldn't believe I hadn't gotten to suck him yet. I loved the sensation of taking a man all the way down, feeling him drive into my throat, but Blake told me that was a treat for a good boy who could follow orders.

I was used to getting what I wanted, and I wasn't going to let him win. If he wanted a compliant boy, then he'd get one. The next time we saw each other, I would transform into the perfect sub. Blake would be impressed, and I'd finally get that fat tail dildo up my ass, and Blake's cock in my mouth instead of a bit. An annoying little voice in my head kept telling me that fake obedience wasn't what Blake wanted. I told that voice to fuck off.

4

BLAKE

"KNEEL by the spanking bench with your hands behind your back."

"Yes, sir," Sean said, the words low and soft. He kept his eyes cast down as he had since I'd opened the door of the private room at Thrust. I watched, mesmerized, as he turned gracefully, walked to the bench, and knelt, hands already clasped behind his back before his knees touched the floor. He didn't prance off, try to surreptitiously touch his cock, or any of the other things I was used to him doing in an attempt to prove he wasn't really submissive.

Either he'd had a complete change of heart in the last few days, or he was acting. My money was on the latter. He wanted a reward, and he was willing to do whatever it took to get it. I had to admire his determination, but I wanted the real Sean with his brattiness and self-indulgence. I'd been willing to be patient, to let him play his games, to give him time to accept what he needed. But maybe I'd been going about this all wrong. Maybe he needed a firmer hand.

I took a deep breath before crossing the room. I was angry, but I needed to act from a place of calm. Thankfully my years as a SEAL had taught me to set aside anger or any other emotion when I had something to accomplish.

"Sean, look at me." When he did, his sickeningly sweet smile would've given him away, even if nothing else had. The only smiles Sean had given me were cheeky ones or ones of pure pleasure.

"That's enough."

"Enough of what, sir?" That fucking wide-eyed innocent look was really testing my patience, but I could do this.

"This pretense of obedience."

"I've done everything you asked, sir. Have I not pleased you?"

That was the best brainwashed sex slave voice I'd ever heard. He'd be perfect in a B-grade sci-fi set on a pleasure planet. "No, you haven't, because this isn't really you. It's not real submission."

"You just said I had to be a good boy."

"I expected the real you to be good."

He laughed, finally breaking character. "That isn't going to happen, but I really want to wear a tail and suck your cock."

"You think you're getting both at the same time?"

He fluttered his lashes. "Aren't I?"

"Not now."

"Because I tried to trick you?"

"Yes."

"So being good is actually being bad?"

On one of my last missions, I'd lain on the ground completely still for six hours even as bugs crawled over me just so I could see if a man returned to his house to collect a package. He hadn't, but I was nowhere near as close to losing my patience then as I was now.

Sean went to all fours and wiggled his ass. "Are you going to spank me now?"

"No."

He dropped to his elbows and arched his back more deeply. "Come on. Punish me since I'm so bad."

"Red."

Sean sat back on his heels and stared at me. "What?"

"Red. I'm not comfortable with where this is going, and I'm too angry to be safe with you."

This time his contrite expression seemed real. "I'm sorry. I was just playing. I thought this was supposed to be a game."

I took a slow breath before speaking. "It is, but it's more too. I want you to have fun, but I also want you to take this seriously. I want you to surrender to me, to let me take care of you and give you what you need. For that to work, we have to trust each other. When you pretend to submit or pretend to like something, that fucks with our trust of each other."

"I told you I couldn't give in to you like that. I'm no good at taking orders."

"You also said you'd trust me to know what you needed."

"I didn't—"

"Please be honest with me."

He looked down then, and his shoulders slumped. "I'm sorry."

"Thank you. Here's the deal. I tried this your way, letting you be bratty, gently correcting you."

"Gently?"

"Trust me, punishments can be much worse than what you've had."

He shivered, and I wasn't sure if it was fear or desire or both.

"I won't do that anymore. Either I start teaching you obedience with your safeword as the only way out, or we stop."

"Stop seeing each other?"

He sounded so fucking lost. Was I doing the wrong thing? I knew what I wanted, and I'd been honest about it from the start. Maybe I should've realized he wasn't capable of accepting it and never started down this path. But I saw potential for things to work. I liked him a lot: his smile, the way he could talk easily about almost anything, and especially those moments when he let his guard down. I wanted to help him do that more.

"I don't want to be trained. That's just… That's not going to work for me. This is a game for me, and that's all."

I nodded. "Do you need anything now, water or for me to stay until you're ready to leave?"

"Um… no… I'm fine."

"Okay." I turned to leave the room. "If you change your mind, you have my number."

"Blake?"

I froze with my hand on the doorknob.

"I'm sorry for how I acted today."

"It's all right. We just want different things. Maybe I've been seeing something that wasn't there."

I left before he could say anything else. My tight hold on my emotions was threatening to give. Apparently I wasn't as invincible as I used to think I was.

5

SEAN

BLAKE WAS WRONG. He'd seen everything clearly. He'd seen deeper into me than anyone else. I was just too scared to admit how right he was. After he left, I pulled my knees up, laid my head on them, and sobbed.

When my tears finally dried up, I considered calling Blake and telling him I did need what he was offering, but I kept seeing the disappointment on his face. He deserved better than me.

I avoided Thrust for several weeks, and when I did go back, I tried my best to avoid Blake.

Avery wanted to know what had happened, but I couldn't talk about it. I was too embarrassed. I'd been a dick, because I was incapable of admitting what I wanted. I told Avery as much of the truth as I could stand: I'd fucked it up, and Blake had left.

I thought I couldn't feel worse. Then Avery fell in love with his best friend Felicity's father-in-law after meeting him at Felicity and Carter's wedding. I watched him give himself to this hot, dominant man without losing himself, or seeming any less of a competent adult. I admired his bravery, even though I teased him mercilessly about his sugar Daddy.

I thought he was just lucky, that he got to be swept away by this amazing man while I was a fucked-up mess, but eventually, I realized Avery was scared too. Scared of how strongly he felt, of how he might screw everything up with Graham. And that made me think he might understand after all why I'd acted like I had with Blake. I wanted to explain what had happened, but what if Avery hated me for hurting Blake? I already worried he'd eventually get tired of putting up with me. I couldn't chance telling him something that might make him decide I wasn't worthy of his friendship.

Avery invited me to go to Thrust with him, his lover Graham, and Graham's friend Leo. Alan was moving to California, and Leo, who owned a similar club in Charlotte, was thinking of buying the club from Alan.

Leo was also hot as fuck, but Avery warned me he was more into obedient pain sluts than brats who wanted nothing to do with whips or knives. Still, I'd followed them around, enjoying the view. We stopped in one of the public play areas to watch a gorgeous man get fisted by his Dom. The combination of fear and lust on the man's face was almost too intense to watch. And when I saw just how far his ass had stretched—yikes. Avery, on the other hand, looked all kinds of intrigued.

A few moments later, Leo indicated he was ready to move on to the next room, which was quieter, a place for those who needed more concentration or wanted fewer onlookers. We turned to follow, and that's when I saw Blake standing in the doorway, looking even taller and hotter than I'd remembered. He wore black leather pants that hugged his muscular thighs and there was a dungeon monitor armband around his perfectly formed bicep. He made the perfect monitor. All he would have to do was look at someone who'd stepped out of line, and they'd be quaking in their—likely outrageous—boots.

Our eyes met, and my stomach knotted. I had to get out of there. I took a step and stumbled. Leo caught my arm as Avery fell into me from behind.

"Are you all right?" Leo asked.

I tried to say something but my throat had gone dry, and I couldn't get any words out. I looked back at the doorway, hoping Blake had gone, but not only was he still there, he was walking toward us. Leo stepped forward to intercept him. I was thankful for that, because I was frozen in place with a sickening combination of fear and longing. I wanted Blake as much as I ever had. Seeing him made me realize nothing had changed. I was a mess, bratty and self-indulgent just like he'd said, and I still didn't have the courage to admit Blake's dominance was exactly what I needed.

I watched as Blake held his hand out to Leo. "I'm Blake. Alan told me you'd be here tonight. He hired me to handle security a few months ago, so he thought you might want to talk to me. I'm monitoring this room tonight, but I'm about to take a break, so we can go somewhere to talk if you'd like."

Blake hadn't actually sought me out. I should be relieved, since I was too scared to talk to him. Instead, I felt disappointed.

"That sounds great," Leo said.

Blake turned to me then. "How've you been?"

I opened my mouth, then closed it and started to back away. My stomach flip-flopped, and I was terrified I was going to be sick right there in front of everyone.

Avery called my name and took a few steps toward me.

Finally, I found my voice. "I... I need to go. I have to..."

Avery whispered something to Graham and then took my arm and pulled me from the room.

"Is that him?" he asked when we were in a quiet hallway. "The man you were going out with?"

I had to swallow before I could answer. "Yes."

Avery frowned. "Are you sure he didn't hurt you?"

"No. It was the other way around."

"You hurt him?"

"Yes. I need to go. I shouldn't have come. I should've known he'd be here." I realized Graham had joined us. He looked as concerned as Avery.

"Did you drive yourself?" Avery asked.

"No, I took an Uber."

"Come on," Graham said as he and Avery each took one of my arms. "We'll walk you out and get you a ride home."

"You don't have to—"

"We're walking you out," Graham insisted, and it reminded me of the way Blake spoke. He had the same air of confidence that people would do as he said. We went through the bar to get to the exit, but when we walked by the booths, I saw Blake, sitting at one with Leo.

I hoped he would ignore me, but before we could scoot past, he stood up. "Sean?"

I squeezed Avery's hand so hard I was surprised he didn't pull away, but at least I didn't run.

"Do you have a minute to talk?" Blake's voice was calm and smooth like usual, but he wasn't holding my gaze and his leg was twitching. I'd never seen him show any sign of nervousness before. If it didn't seem ridiculous, I'd think he was scared.

"I… I don't…"

"Talk to him," Leo said, standing to join us.

"You might feel better if you do." Avery kept his voice low.

"I've never seen you sadder than the day you ended things with him."

Blake held out his hand, and I wanted to take it, to go with him.

How much longer are you going to deny what you want, what you need?

I'm not ready.

You'll never be ready. You have to talk to him anyway.

I wiped my sweaty hand on my jeans and reached for Blake, trying to ignore that I was visibly shaking.

He tugged on my hand until I was by his side.

6

BLAKE

I PUSHED through the swinging door that led down a hallway to bathrooms as well as a storage room and a few offices.

"You're not expecting a bathroom BJ, right?" Sean asked.

I looked back at him. "One thing I can assure you is that we will never have sex in a club bathroom."

He grinned. "I'm cool with that."

"Good. At least that's one thing we agree on."

"So where are we going?"

"I'm taking you to an office the security officers use when they need to question someone. It's private, but it allows me to still be on the premises since I'm supposed to be on duty. Once we're there, I'll see if I can find someone to take over my DM job for a while so we can talk."

"You don't have to do that."

"I want to."

"Okay." Sean seemed more resigned than eager to talk to me, but at least he no longer looked terrified.

When we reached the office, I unlocked it and motioned for Sean to enter first. He sat down in one of the folding chairs, and I chose the one beside him, rather than in the more comfortable seat behind the desk. I didn't want him to think I was trying to intimidate him.

I sent off a quick text asking one of my security experts who was there that night if he could watch the quiet room for half an hour. Then I looked at Sean. "How about we start over?"

Sean frowned. "Wh-what do you mean?"

I held out my hand. "Hi. I'm Blake."

"Oh, that kind of starting over." He took my hand and smiled. "I love how your hands are so warm. I mean… I'm Sean. Shit. I suck at this game."

He was adorable when he was flustered like this. "It's nice to meet you, Sean."

"It's… um… nice to meet you too?"

"Is it?" I wanted him to be sure.

He nodded. "Yes. It is. Very."

I shifted in my seat so I was facing him more fully. "What are you looking for tonight?"

"You're very direct."

"Not really. Direct would be saying I'd like to put you on your knees and teach you how to please me. I thought that might be a bit much."

He licked his lips. "Maybe. I mean if it really were… Or maybe not?"

"You seem uncertain. Am I making you nervous?"

"No. Yes. It's okay. I'm here to find out if I'm compatible with someone. Someone I've been watching for a while."

I nodded. "Anyone I might know?"

"He's tall, really tall, and strong. Like he could probably deadlift my car."

Somehow I managed not to laugh. "That's impressive."

He nodded. "I think he knows how impressive he is, but he's not arrogant about it except when he expects submission from someone."

39

I let my gaze slide over him. "Do you like arrogant men?"

He chewed his lip for a second, then said, "Yeah."

"A lot of guys wouldn't admit that."

"I wouldn't have a few weeks ago."

That was encouraging. "I see." I cleared my throat and continued, "How would you go about finding out if you and this man are compatible?"

He shrugged. "I'm not sure. What would you suggest?"

"Hmm. I think sometimes we get it wrong, because we jump right into a list of negotiations. That's fine if all you're looking for is a scene, but if you think things might develop into more than that, maybe you should start the same way vanilla people do."

"By talking?" Sean asked.

"No, by kissing."

"Oh… I like kissing."

"I'm glad to hear that. Would you like to try it, to practice, you know, in case you meet this man tonight?"

"I… I think I might have met him already."

"Really?"

He nodded.

"That's good to hear."

I scooted my chair closer and cupped his face. Sean held still, and I could feel the tension in him. I hoped it came from desire, not fear.

"Relax. I'm going to take this slow. I don't have any expectations tonight, okay?"

"Okay."

I leaned closer, but instead of kissing him, I nuzzled his neck, breathing deeply and drawing in his scent. I nipped at him, and he jumped.

"Do you like that?" I asked, mouth right against the outer edge of his ear.

"Y-yes."

I did it again, biting down harder this time.

"Please." The whine in his voice shot straight to my cock.

I licked and sucked at his neck, working my way down to the curve of his shoulder where I bit down harder, making him gasp. My cock was begging me to go faster, and my pants had gotten very uncomfortable.

Sean pulled me to him, seeming even more impatient than I was. I kissed him, forcing his lips apart and pushing my tongue into him the way I wanted to push my cock into his ass. He held onto my waist, seeming to need an anchor. I let the kiss go on and on, longer than I'd kissed anyone in forever.

When Sean finally pulled away, eyes wide, breath ragged, I urged him onto my lap. He groaned as he straddled me and our cocks touched. I felt a jolt of need, even through the layers of fabric. And it was clear he felt the same.

I held his gaze, using what he called my Dom magic. I heard his sharp intake of breath, but I didn't breathe at all, I just took in the want in his eyes. Then I yanked him to me and kissed him again as he rolled his hips, pushing our cocks together.

I growled, and he thrust harder.

"Want you. Please."

I forced myself to break the kiss, gripping his shoulders and pushing gently. "We need to slow down. We're just making out, getting to know each other."

"But I want you." The whine in his voice was too fucking cute.

"I know you do, but I have conditions."

He groaned. "I thought we were starting over."

"We are. Pretend you've never heard these conditions before." He started to speak, but I laid a finger over his lips. "Just listen."

He shifted off my lap and settled back in his chair. I took his hands and studied him, trying to read his thoughts.

"Do they teach you that in SEAL school?"

I couldn't help but smile. "Teach me what?"

"That staring thing where it's like you can see all my secrets."

I wasn't sure I wanted that much power. "I'm just trying to gauge your reactions and make sure I have your attention."

"Trust me. You have my attention."

"Good. I want you to submit to me. I want to put you on your knees, not because I get off on forcing you, but because I want to give you pleasure, to let you relax and be free." I scooted closer so I could massage his shoulders. "I want to make all this tension melt away. I want to take care of you, but to do that, I need you to listen to me, even when that's hard for you."

"How will you do that? Melt the tension, I mean."

"First, you need to tell me what you want to learn."

Color rushed to his face, and he looked away.

"Sean, I won't judge you. No matter what you tell me."

"You said I was a brat."

"I did, but a lot of men love bratty subs."

"Not you, though?"

I was starting to reevaluate my feelings on that. "I like a challenge. I don't mind a bratty sub, but I want him to be willing to learn discipline."

"And that's why you want to teach me."

"Yes, but I also think you'd be happier if you had someone keeping you in line."

He sighed. "Everyone thinks I'm a child, but I—"

I took hold of his chin and forced him to look at me. "I don't think that, Sean. I think you're an adult, who has some habits he'd like to change and needs some extra guidance and care to do that. There's nothing wrong with that and nothing wrong with you for needing it."

"It's still embarrassing."

I looked down pointedly at his cock, which hadn't lost any of its enthusiasm as we'd talked. "I think sometimes you like being embarrassed."

His cheeks got even redder. "Maybe. But why do you still want this after I was such an asshole to you?"

"Because I know you were scared."

"I was, but I'm a mess. I never get anywhere on time, and Avery has to remind me of things constantly. I can't settle on a career. I want you to make me behave, to discipline me. I love how it feels to give in to you, but I fight it, because I don't like the idea of giving up control."

"You will never lose control over anything with me. The submissive is the one who decides what happens. If you use your safeword, I'll stop immediately, no matter what the reason is. If you say no to a scene I propose, we won't do it. You always have control. I'm guiding you through the experience, not forcing you."

"But don't you get off on controlling me? Isn't that like the point?"

"I love knowing a man trusts me enough to surrender to me, and I love when they obey my commands, but more than controlling them, I want the high of knowing I've cared for them and given pleasure."

"I thought you special forces types liked to dominate everyone."

I raised my brows. "Seriously?"

He sighed. "I know that's a stereotype and probably ridiculous, but you certainly look the part."

I rolled my eyes. "I guess I do, but trust me, if you want to control things, the last thing you should do is become a SEAL. You go where your orders take you and learn to be ready for absolutely anything. The only thing you can be sure of on a mission is that nothing will go as planned."

"Wow. I… Yeah, I can see that. Sorry."

"It's all right. I can't blame you when so many books and movies get it wrong."

"Would I get a spanking for saying that if we were playing tonight?"

I studied him for a moment, wanting to make him squirm. "You seem very eager to be spanked, but I'm not sure that's what you need. I would punish you somehow, though."

"Like when you wouldn't let me come, because I was late. Or, I mean, if I was late—"

"You don't have to keep pretending you don't know me. That was just to get us started."

"Okay. I'm still not sure I can be what you want."

"You don't have to change yourself to be what I want. You just have to be willing to be honest and try."

He nodded, still looking nervous and unsure.

"I don't want you to decide tonight, anyway. I want you to take at least a week and think about it."

"Oh. I guess I can do that."

"Good, but before you go—"

"Go?"

"Yes. I said we'd make out and then talk. We've done that."

"But…"

I shook my head. "That's all I'm offering now."

"Fine."

I couldn't help but smile at his disgusted tone.

"Are you thinking up ways to train that kind of response out of me?"

"Maybe."

"So what did you want to tell me before you send me off with blue balls?'

"I want you to understand clearly what I'm proposing."

44

His expression was wary. "Okay."

"You will agree to follow the rules I set for you during a scene and when you're home."

He frowned. "What kind of rules would I have at home? Stuff like having to be on time and having to clean up?"

"Yes, and sometimes I'll order you not to jerk off or watch porn. Things like that."

He groaned. "Seriously?"

"Yes. You'll agree to follow my rules, and when you don't, I'll punish you. When we're together, I'll help you work on your self-discipline."

"Like with the pony play?"

"Yes. It's a good way to train you to obey lots of commands. And once you get into your role as a ponyboy, it might be easier for you to surrender."

"Letting go like that scares me."

I squeezed his hand. "Thank you for being honest. And you don't have to do any of this if you don't think it's right for you. All I can do is guess your needs. I could be wrong."

He shook his head. "You're not. But I'm still scared."

"Even if I'm right, you don't have to agree to this. It's your choice."

"I have to do this if I want you, though."

"If you want more than friendship, this is what I have to offer. But I could help you find someone who could give you whatever you want. I know a few Doms who love casual play with bratty subs."

He shook his head. "I want you. I… um… I like you. I haven't even wanted to fuck anyone since I was with you."

I hadn't expected that. "Really?"

He nodded and said, "And trust me. This has been a record dry spell for me. I've been jerking off about ten times a day, mostly thinking about you and that damn bridle and tail."

I grinned. He was fucking perfect. If only he could find the courage to give in to what he needed.

"You've got nothing to say to that? No confessions of your own?"

I could tell he needed me to be vulnerable now, so I gave him what he needed. "I've fantasized about you constantly since the first time I saw you bent over and being spanked while you shook your ass and begged for more. Nothing, not you fighting me, not you laughing when I wanted to be serious, has stopped you showing up in all my fantasies. How's that for a confession?"

His eyes were wide as he stared at me. "That's… um… wow."

"Go home and think about what I've proposed."

"You're sure you won't compromise, you could just spank me and then—"

"No. That's not going to work for us, and I think you know that. I want more than just spanking and fucking. I want a relationship."

"You mean like we'll go on dates and talk and stuff?"

He really was such a fucking mess. "Yes. Is that a deal breaker?"

"Um… I don't… Maybe."

I raised my brows and held his gaze.

"Not the talking or whatever, but I don't do relationships." He rolled his eyes as soon as the words were out. "Ugh. I sound like a douche, don't I?"

I nodded. "You kind of do."

"I have reasons for being like that."

"Do you want to talk about them?"

He shook his head. "Not now. Probably not for a long time."

"All right. That can wait."

"So it's all or nothing?" he asked, still looking hopeful that I'd change my mind.

"It is. It hurt when you tried to fake your submission. I don't want to go through something like that again."

"I shouldn't have done that. I was awful, and I can't believe you still want to try this."

I took his hands in mine and held his gaze. "I want this, but I want clear rules between us."

"I guess that's fair."

"So you'll think about it?"

He nodded.

"For at least a week?"

"Yes, sir."

I scowled at him, thinking he was mocking me.

"I actually meant that. It's hard not to say 'sir' to you."

I couldn't help but smile. "I've heard that before."

"I bet you have. Should I go now?"

"Yes. Would you like me to walk you out?"

"Um... Yeah, I would."

We both stood, and I offered him my arm like an old-fashioned gentleman.

He rolled his eyes, but he took it anyway, and I walked him out, praying he'd call me in a week and say yes.

7

SEAN

THE THURSDAY after The Night of Seeing Blake Again, Avery and I were watching *Bridget Jones*. Avery had to call Graham, but I kept the movie running since we both had it memorized.

But when he came to the couch, I hit pause. He wasn't smiling like he usually did whenever he and Graham talked. After he explained that he'd be going to Charlotte to see Graham that weekend instead of Graham coming here, he said, "I want to talk to you about something."

"Okay."

"But you have to be serious. I feel weird talking to Felicity since Graham's her father-in-law, but I need to know you won't laugh at me."

"Are you going to confess to some kinky shit you're doing?" As if I had any room to talk.

"I call him Daddy, and he calls me boy, and I totally get off on it. There. That's out of the way."

I made a strangled sound and tried my best not to give myself away. Avery had told me before how hot he thought

Daddy kink was, and I acted all squicked out. He still thought I was against it.

"But that's not what I wanted to say."

Avery seemed so uncertain, I thought it might help if I shared too. It was way past time. "If we're doing confessions, I tried pony play with Blake, but he said I didn't have enough discipline. He wants to teach me how to be obedient, and I kind of want him to, but he scares me."

Avery frowned. "He scares you because he's so dominant?"

I shook my head.

"Then why?"

"I feel too much when I'm with him. I want to give him everything he asks for, not just because it's hot, but because I want to please him. I want him to fix the mess I've made of my life, but it's wrong to depend on someone like that."

"Are you sure it's wrong if it's what you both want? Maybe it would be good for you."

Having an older man care for him had certainly been good for Avery. Could it really be okay to accept what Blake was offering? "I don't know. Don't I just need to man up and be an adult?"

Avery huffed. "Like that ever works. Look, you can be a mess, but you're hardly failing at adulting. You pay your rent on time, and even though you keep changing career paths, you take what you're doing seriously. You're a capable adult, despite eating Captain Crunch or Cocoa Puffs for dinner half the time. That's your choice. Whatever you might do with Blake won't change that."

I wanted to believe him, but that was part of the problem. It would be all too easy to just say yes. I'd spent too many years taking the easy way out. "I asked him if we could just go out casually, do some scenes, enjoy each other, but either we do this his way or not at all."

"So he won't compromise?"

I shook my head. "I can't blame him for that, though. It's because I hurt him." I took a deep breath. The rest of what I had to say scared me the most. "Blake told me he wanted to be serious, and I laughed at him and then told him to just get on with it and spank me. He called an end to our scene, and that's when we stopped seeing each other."

Instead of getting angry with me, Avery took my hand and squeezed it. "If you're interested in him, and you do seem to be, then at least think about whether his way could work. And if not, maybe if he sees you're willing to try, you can find a compromise then. You just have to be honest about what you're feeling."

Wow. Graham really had been good for him. "Listen to you, Mr. Maturity."

"Nothing like sage relationship advice from an expert who's been in one two-month-long relationship with his best friend's father-in-law."

"Exactly." God, I loved this man. I was so lucky he'd been willing to put up with me for so many years. I pulled him to me for a tight hug. "I'm sorry. I totally derailed our conversation with my confession."

"Did it feel good to finally talk about Blake?"

"Yeah. It did. I was worried you'd be pissed at me for how I treated him."

Avery frowned. "I don't expect you to be perfect. If you didn't care that you'd hurt him, if you weren't worried about it, then I'd be mad. But you admitted you fucked up, which shows me you're exactly who I thought you were, even if you pretend to be a heartless asshole sometimes."

The problem was I thought I was a heartless asshole most of the time, and Blake deserved better than that.

The next day, I came home to a silent apartment. Avery had left to spend the weekend with Graham, lucky bastard. He'd be fucked in every room of Graham's no doubt enormous house. And probably in the back yard too.

I was horny, bored, and lonely, and that was a terrible combination. I opened the fridge and surveyed the contents. Nothing looked appealing. Should I order takeout and sit on the couch stuffing my face or go out by myself?

I could call Blake. It had been exactly a week.

I remembered how soft his voice had been when he'd talked to me that night at Thrust. It was obvious he was working hard not to spook me or seem like he was pushing me.

When I'd first let him lead me away from Avery and Graham, I'd wanted to beg him to take me home, to fuck me thoroughly. I wanted him to make me do his bidding, to take all my choices away, but that wouldn't have gotten us anywhere. If he'd done it, I would've run when it was over and still refused to admit how much I loved it. Of course Blake knew that talking to me, making me think it over was the only way he'd get a truthful confession out of me.

Was I ready to give him what he wanted?

Avery thought I should call Blake. He hadn't said that outright, but I could tell he did, and I wanted to but...

No. I was done being afraid, done being a mess and not doing anything about it.

As if to illustrate just how much I needed a Daddy, it took me a while to find my phone, because it had fallen out of my pocket in my car and was still lying there on the seat. I shivered as I wondered how Blake might punish me for that.

"Hi, Sean," Blake said when he answered after the second ring.

"Hi."

"Any particular reason you're calling?"

"Um… it's been a week since I saw you."

"It has." Damn his cool self-control.

"I… I want to see you again."

"You want to see me again, or you want to accept my offer?" I should have known he'd make me say it explicitly.

I took a deep breath and let it out slowly. I could do this. "I want to accept your offer."

"Can you be at my house at seven tomorrow night?"

I wanted to tell him I was available to be there right that second. Instead, I just said, "Yes."

"Good. We'll have dinner, and then I'll have few challenges for you."

I swallowed hard. "Challenges?"

"Yes. Are there any foods you're allergic to or just don't eat?"

"I don't have any allergies, and I basically eat anything unless Avery or I tried to cook it."

He laughed. "I'll remember not to ask you to cook for me."

"That's good." Blake didn't say anything else. Sometimes I hated how comfortable he was with silence. "So… um… I guess I'll see you tomorrow."

"I'm looking forward to it."

"Me too."

I was about to end the call when he said, "Sean?"

"Yes?"

"No jerking off. The next time you come will be with me."

My hand had already been on my dick. "What? I can't—"

"Sean."

"Yes, sir. No touching."

"That's much better. I know you can be a good boy."

I could, but he wouldn't know, would he?

"I'll know if you disobey, and you won't like the consequences."

"Shit. How do you read my mind like that?"

"It's not all that hard with you."

I wanted to argue, but he was probably right. "I'm either thinking about getting off or about how to defy you."

"Exactly, but tonight you're going to think about obeying me so you can be rewarded. Bad boys don't get to come."

"Yes, sir."

"I like how sincere that sounded." I could hear the smile in his voice.

"I'm trying."

"I know you are. And I appreciate it. It means a lot that you're willing to accept my conditions."

"Thank you, sir. I'll see you tomorrow."

"See you then."

When I ended the call, my heart was pounding, and the room swam around me. I'd actually agreed to be his submissive, and now I had to take it seriously. I wasn't going to hurt Blake again. I'd promised him something, and I was going to follow through. Or at least I was going to try, because I wanted to please him more than I'd ever wanted anything.

8

BLAKE

WHEN I'D THOUGHT about what I would say if Sean actually called me, I'd originally planned to ask him about his favorite restaurant and take him out to dinner. But I'd decided that cooking for him was better. I could show him I was serious about wanting to take care of him. I wasn't an amazing cook, but I was good with basic recipes, and my lasagna was always a hit. So I went with that. I made a salad and had garlic bread ready to go in the oven.

I checked the lasagna and glanced at the clock. He would be here any minute, unless he was late. I was really hoping he wouldn't be. As much as punishment could be enjoyable for both of us, I didn't want him to start with a strike against him. The doorbell interrupted my thoughts. I tossed the oven mitt on the counter and rushed across my apartment, though I forced myself to slow down and take a breath before opening the door. I didn't want to appear insanely eager.

"I'm on time," Sean said, practically bouncing.

"You are."

"That's good, right?"

He seemed so earnest, I bit back a laugh. "Yes, that's good."

"I want to get this right."

"You already are. Come in."

He did, and I closed the door behind him.

"As long as you're here because you want to be, as long as you're being real with me, then you're doing everything I asked. I don't expect you to be perfect. I don't want you to stop being you, and if that's what you thought—"

"No, I didn't, but I hurt you before."

I nodded. He knew it was true. I wasn't going to deny it.

"I don't want to do that again."

I smiled. "Then I don't think you will."

"Why do you trust me?"

"Because you apologized. You showed you care about how I feel. You're not just using me to get off or so you can brag that you've been with a SEAL."

He fidgeted for a moment, then said, "I did think about how cool the SEAL thing was. I mean…"

"I think anybody would, and you are very lucky to get all this." I swept a hand down my body.

"Wow. So humble."

"It's one of my best qualities."

"Does that happen a lot?" he asked. "Guys wanting you just to check off 'fucked a SEAL' on their bucket list?"

"Yes, but let's not talk about that now. Come on into the kitchen. The lasagna is probably done, so once I put the garlic bread in for a few minutes, dinner will be ready."

"You made dinner?"

Heat rushed to my face, and I was sure I was blushing, a rare thing for me. "I did. I thought it would be nice to just stay here instead of going out. I hope that's okay." I couldn't remember ever being this nervous with a guy.

"It's great. I just can't believe you did that for me."

"Don't get too excited. I have a few standard dinners in my repertoire and that's the extent of my skill set."

"I can hardly make toast, so I'm seriously impressed."

"You might want to taste it before you praise me."

He shook his head. "It smells fantastic. I'm sure it will be great. And far better than the ramen or cheap pizza I would've had if I hadn't come over tonight."

I gestured toward the table. "Have a seat."

"I don't mind helping."

I shook my head. "No. I'm doing this for you."

"Aren't I supposed to serve you?"

"This isn't scene space. We're just talking and having dinner."

"Like a regular date?"

"Yes, like a date anyone might have." I hoped my answer wouldn't spook him.

"Like one with people who arrive on time without the threat of orgasm denial?"

A laugh burst from me. "Yes, just like that." Still chuckling, I asked, "What would you like to drink? I've got Coke, Diet Coke, orange San Pellegrino, club soda, Asheville City tap water."

He grinned. "Diet Coke would be great."

I grabbed a can from the fridge and handed it to him. "I would offer wine, but—" Mixing alcohol with the kind of play I had planned was a bad idea.

He shook his head. "It's not even just a safe, sane, consensual thing for me. I learned the hard way that drinking and hooking up don't mix for me."

Ice-cold anger crackled through me at the thought of someone hurting him. I had to take a deep breath before I could unclench my fists.

"Are you about to go all overprotective on me?" Sean asked.

"I want to take care of you, and that means protecting you."

I thought he would protest, but he just smiled. "All right. If you insist."

"I do. Do you want to talk about what happened?"

"It was several years ago, and I don't know the guys' names or even whether one or both of them were responsible, so don't think about trying to go after them or anything."

I wanted to argue, to tell him I could track someone down with the tiniest bit of information, but I didn't. I just said, "Okay."

"I remember being at a bar, chatting with some guys. I was drunk, really drunk. I have a vague memory of agreeing to go home with them and getting in a car, but after that, I don't know what happened. I woke up tied to a bed with the feeling gone in my hands. Two guys were passed out on the bed with me. With tugging and some use of my teeth, I managed to free myself. Then I got dressed and got the hell out of there."

"You should've pressed charges."

"For all I know, I consented to everything."

"If you were too drunk to remember it the next day, you were too drunk to consent. They should never have touched you."

"I know. I just… It's in the past, and now I'm more careful."

I knelt beside his chair, not wanting him to feel as if I were looming over him as I spoke. "I will never ask for your submission when I'm drinking, okay? If you want to hang out and drink together, that's fine. We can even fool around, but I will never ask you for anything."

His expression softened, and he smiled. "Can I kiss you?"

"Yes." He leaned forward and brushed his lips across mine. I deepened the kiss, but only for a moment.

He pouted when I sat back with no further contact.

"After dinner you'll have a chance to earn more."

"I don't like waiting."

"I've noticed." The timer rang, letting me know the garlic bread was done. "Stay right there, and I'll bring our plates."

S ean groaned when he took his first bite of lasagna, and I had to ignore my body's reaction to the sound.

"This is so good," he said. "Why'd you try to act like you can't cook?"

"I didn't say I couldn't cook, I said I could only do basic, no-frills stuff."

"This is plenty of frills for me," he said, reaching for his garlic bread.

He didn't say anything else as we continued to eat, and I noticed that despite him enjoying the food, he was fidgety. He hadn't looked at me since he'd exclaimed over the lasagna.

"Are you all right?" I asked.

He frowned. "Sure. Why?"

"You're a lot quieter than usual."

"Oh… um… I can talk if you want me to."

"You don't have to, but I want to make sure you're comfortable."

"No. I mean, I'm fine. So like, what do you do when you're not stalking around Thrust looking like everyone's fantasy military man or literally whipping subs into shape?"

He was nervous, there was no doubt about that, but I no longer thought he was truly freaking out. "Flogging subs, yes, but I've never learned how to use a whip. That's a little too intense for me."

Sean shivered. "Me too. I'm all for hands or a belt or a riding crop, but that's about it."

"I have plenty of ideas for things to use on your ass, but

none of them will break the skin, and I'll always check with you first."

He smiled then, seeming more at ease. "I know. I really do trust you."

"I'm glad. As far as what else I do, my business takes most of my time between doing security for events. We do consulting, and there's way more paperwork than any movie ever shows. Most of the time I love it, but other than working out and occasionally visiting Thrust, I haven't made time for much else."

"That kind of sucks, but you're seeing me now. Avery would say that was work too, but you could at least count training undisciplined men as a hobby, right?"

That was the snarky Sean I was used to. "You might be work, but at least I won't have to keep records on you and constantly update spreadsheets."

"True. Do you have an office assistant or something?"

"I have someone who helps me part time with the office work, but there are some things I just have to do myself. I guess I'm sort of a control freak."

"I knew it," he shouted, nearly leaping out of his seat.

I glared at him with mock annoyance. "Not as a Dom, but with my business. And" —I sighed— "okay, fine, with other things too. I like to be in control, but I don't want a slave. I want you to be you, and to be here because you want to be."

"I am. I've enjoyed everything we've done. When you push and challenge me, I love it, even if I shouldn't."

"Who says you shouldn't?"

He shrugged. "I don't know. It's just… I don't want to depend on someone."

"Sean, you do realize that you deserve to be happy, right?"

He looked down at his plate and moved a stray noodle around.

"Talk to me."

"Avery says I use my brattiness as a defense, because I'm scared of liking someone or something that might end up disappointing me."

"And what do you say?"

"I think he's right. It's a lot easier to try something out and then move on. If nothing really matters to me, I can't end up being stuck in a situation that makes me unhappy."

"And this applies to both relationships and other things in your life, like your job?"

He nodded.

"I guess it's easier in some ways, but is it satisfying?"

Sean scowled at me. "Are you like a closet romantic?"

"I'm not in the closet. I think everyone deserves to be loved."

"So you're hoping to find the love of your life?"

I knew we were on shaky ground here, but I wanted to be as honest as I could. "Do you think that's wrong?"

"Not unless you expect me to… I just can't take that kind of pressure."

"All I expect is for you to follow our agreement. If you decide you want more, then we can talk about that."

He looked shaken. Maybe I should've played off the whole romance thing as a joke. "Sean, if you've changed your mind—"

"No, I haven't, but this thing between us has to be about submission and sex. I can't do more."

"Look at me."

He did. "Take a deep breath." When we both had, I continued. "I'm not asking for more than that. I won't try to take more than you can give, okay?"

"Okay." His voice was steadier now.

"Do you still want to play tonight?"

He nodded. "Yes, please."

When we'd finished eating and cleared the table, I took

his hand and led him to my bedroom. "Are you ready to begin?"

"Totally."

I raised my brows. "Try again."

He cleared his throat. "Yes, sir. I'm ready."

"Better. Strip and kneel by my bed."

He followed my orders eagerly, probably anticipating a spanking or some other enjoyable torment. I fought the urge to smile, knowing how much he would hate what I actually had planned.

"Good boy. You may sit back on your heels or be up on your knees, whichever is more comfortable for you, but you're going to be there a while."

"Wh-why?"

"I'm going to clean up the kitchen, and you're going to wait here for me. You're not to get up, and you may not touch yourself. Is that clear?"

"I… Yes, sir."

"Good. If you need to stop, use your safeword. Otherwise I'll expect to find you here when I'm ready to return."

I could almost hear the swirl of questions in his mind. The tension in his shoulders let me know how hard this was for him. His cock was hard, and precum beaded at the tip. On impulse, I stepped forward and swiped my finger across his slit, capturing a bead of liquid. I brought my finger to my mouth and sucked it clean. He watched me, eyes wide.

"Mmm, you taste so good."

His mouth opened like he was going to speak, but I saved him from disobeying by saying, "I'll be back. Be a good boy."

9

SEAN

WHAT THE HELL was I doing here, kneeling all alone when I could be at Thrust with a cock driving into me or at least a hand cracking across my ass, getting me all heated up. I could easily have found someone to make me come from a combination of embarrassment, pain, and hot fucking.

I didn't like admitting how much I liked a bit of humiliation, nothing serious, just a hot public spanking or being used like I was nothing but a hole. Kneeling on Blake's floor, aching to come while he ignored me, was doing it for me. It wasn't like he'd tied me up or anything. I could just stand up and walk away, but I was choosing to stay, and the shame I felt from that only made me hornier. I wanted him so badly, I was willing to let him force me to earn every orgasm he gave me.

I heard water running and the clatter of plates, then a sound that must have been a dishwasher opening. I tried to remember how many things had been piled up in the kitchen. It hadn't looked very messy. Maybe he'd be done soon.

My feet were starting to tingle from sitting back on my

heels, so I raised up on my knees and shifted a bit. I didn't dare move too much though. I was determined to show him I could do exactly what he asked.

A few moments later, the water turned off, and I sighed in relief when he walked into the bedroom. Then he held up a butt plug and a riding crop. The plug was not one with a tail. It was about the size of an average cock, nothing intimidating, but it likely meant I wasn't about to get Blake inside me, which was what I really wanted. Well, that and for him to spank me with that delicious crop.

Blake laid a hand on my shoulder and knelt behind me. "I thought you might need an extra challenge now that you've adjusted to waiting."

"But I thought—"

"Every time you speak out of turn, I add to your time on your knees."

"Fuck."

He gave me an evil grin. "You must enjoy kneeling for me."

I pressed my lips together, holding in all the names I wanted to call him, and the questions I had. Was he really going to leave me here longer? With the plug inside me?

He ran a hand down my spine, which made me shiver. Then he spoke with his lips nearly touching my ear. "May I plug your ass?"

"Yes, sir." I forced the words out, though I wanted to tell him to fuck off. Or beg for his dick. Or both.

"I always sterilize any toys I'm using in a scene, but if you'd feel more comfortable, I'll put a condom on it."

"I trust you, sir."

"Thank you, boy."

I heard the unmistakable sound of him slicking up the plug. "Now lean forward and present your ass to me."

I did what he said, because I'd promised to obey, and I

was determined to take what he gave. But the idea of kneeling there with my ass stuffed was hotter than I'd ever admit to him.

"Can you take this without prep?" he asked as he rubbed my hole with the tip of the plug.

I nodded. It would hurt, but I could do it.

"When I ask you a question, I want to hear your answer."

"Yes, sir, I can take it." I wanted that sting to help me forget the ache in my balls.

He pushed the plug into me, moving slowly, but not stopping until the base met my ass. By then I was panting, my ass stretched and burning, my dick begging for more. I wanted to be fucked, pounded, owned. This fullness was nowhere near enough.

"Good boy." He kissed the base of my spine. "You took that so well."

I nodded, and he slapped my ass so hard I cried out.

"Thank me properly."

"Th-thank you, sir. I wanted to take it for you, sir."

"Much better. Now come back onto your knees. I have some work to do now."

Wasn't he going to use the crop on me?

As if he'd heard me, he laid the crop down on the floor in front of me. "This is for later. I expect you to follow the same rules you had before."

I bit my lip to keep from protesting and earning even more time before he would give me some relief. I studied the pictures on Blake's dresser. There were several of him and men I guessed were part of his SEAL team and one with an older woman who looked so much like him she had to be his mom. Sadly, that distraction only lasted a few seconds. How much longer would he leave me here?

The plug seemed to be taunting me. No matter what I did I couldn't stop thinking about how it was there, holding me open, filling me, but not giving me the stimulation I craved. I wasn't sure I could last much longer before I broke and touched my cock. Surely Blake would come back soon.

I stayed still for what felt like ages. I was sweating with the effort it took not to move when my body was begging me to. I wiggled my hips just a little and the plug pressed on my prostate, making me gasp. I prayed Blake hadn't heard. After that, I tried to focus on my breathing like I did when Avery dragged me to yoga class. I counted my inhale and then tried to exhale for double that count. I paused before inhaling again and repeated the process.

When Blake entered the room, he startled me. Apparently, the breathing exercise had worked.

"You've done very well, boy. I'm proud of you."

"Thank you, sir." The words came more easily this time.

"You've earned a reward, but first" —He paused to pick up the crop— "We need to talk about your behavior this week. Have you done anything you need to be punished for?"

"Um… I'm not sure, sir."

"Were you late to work or to meet friends? Did you clean up after yourself?"

I looked down, not wanting to tell him.

"Sean, if you don't tell me, I'll have to guess. I might assume you've been much worse than you have, since I really like how your ass looks all red from my belt."

Fuck. "Um… I was supposed to move Avery's laundry to the dryer, but I forgot and it got really gross."

He nodded. "And?"

Why did I think I could get away with just that? "I was late to work on Thursday."

"Why?"

Oh, shit. "Do you really need—" His look silenced my protest. Heat filled my face as I said, "I was jacking off."

He coughed a bit, or maybe he was laughing. "What did you say?"

I'd whispered the words, but I was sure he'd heard them.

"And you had to do that before work?"

"Yes?"

"No."

Of course he was right. "No, sir. I didn't."

"Head to the ground, ass up. I'm going to crop your ass to help you remember how to be a good boy."

"Yes, sir."

The first slap of the crop landed on the base of the plug, driving it against my prostate. I gasped.

"Whatever you do, don't come," he said.

"I… Please."

He hit the plug again and heat seared through me. I couldn't take much more of that, but he seemed to know, because after that he mostly brought the crop down on my ass. It stung so badly, and I was whimpering and writhing by the time he gave me a final hard slap. I lay there trying to catch my breath and fighting the tears that had once again gathered during my punishment.

Blake stroked my back. "Good boy. You did so good."

"Th-thank you, sir."

"Are you ready for your reward now?"

"Yes, sir."

He helped me to my feet and held onto me since I was unsteady. "I'm going to fuck your mouth, and you get to choose how you want it. You can kneel or sit or lay on the bed with your head hanging over the edge."

I knew a lot of guys wouldn't think that was a reward, but I'd been hungry for his cock for ages, and I was thrilled. "Thank you, sir. I want to lie on the bed. I love to have my face fucked like that."

He smiled. "Go on and get into position."

I climbed onto the bed, trying to ignore how every movement jiggled the plug. When I was situated, Blake came to stand by my head. I watched as he unzipped his pants and pulled out his thick cock. I couldn't wait to have him push it into my throat.

He leaned over me, letting the tip almost touch my lips. Instinctively, I knew I was supposed to stay still and let him control everything.

"I want to hold your arms down. Would you like that?"

I nodded enthusiastically, which made me dizzy. "Yes, sir."

"Good." He held up a small red ball. "This has a bell in it. Hold it in your hand and shake or toss it if you need me to stop."

"Yes, sir." I took the ball from him and gripped it tightly.

He wrapped his fingers around my upper arms, pinning me to the mattress. "Good boy. Now open your mouth so I can use it."

When he pushed his cock in, I tongued the veiny underside. He thrust deeper, and I swallowed around him and hummed.

"I like that, boy. You're good at this."

I smiled around his cock.

"Are you ready for all of me?"

I nodded, hoping he saw how eager I was.

He must have, because he drove in all the way and held himself there until I was almost out of air. He pulled out when I started to struggle, but he went right back in after I'd sucked in a breath. He kept fucking me, hard and deep.

I handled it well at first, but as his thrusts sped up, I struggled to breathe. I gagged and sputtered and fought him, trying to free my arms, but he held me down easily. I'd never had a man use my mouth this hard, and it was glorious.

I couldn't touch myself with my arms restrained, but I was right on the edge of coming hands free. I tried to hold myself back, but with his cock choking me, I needed my concentration to keep breathing.

My balls were tight. I was too close, but then Blake shouted, "Take it, take my whole load."

His cum flooded my throat. I swallowed again and again. Focusing on his orgasm helped me stop my own.

When he pulled out, he cupped my chin and looked down at me. "Are you okay?"

"Yes," I croaked, my voice barely there.

"Are you sure?"

I smiled as I nodded. My face was sticky with sweat, drool, and snot. My cock ached and a single touch might make me come, but I was happier than I'd been in ages.

"That was amazing, boy. Now it's your turn."

He reached for my cock and started jerking me off.

I whimpered. "It's okay, boy, you can come."

"Thank you. Thank you."

Seconds later, I was shooting over my chest, but he kept working me until I'd softened and it started to hurt.

"Feel better?"

"Y-yes, sir." I wasn't sure how I got the words out.

"Here." He helped me scoot farther onto the bed so my head was supported. "I'm going to get something to clean you up. And then I'll massage your neck so you're not stiff."

"Thank you, sir."

"Later I'll make you some tea for your throat."

I smiled at him, feeling floaty and peaceful. What did it say about me that being held down and face-fucked brought me inner peace?

Blake washed my face and neck and then asked me to turn over, so he could give me a massage. By the time he stopped, I was almost asleep.

He helped me sit up, then he cupped my face and gave me a kiss that was as sweet as what we'd just done was filthy.

"You're welcome to use my shower. And you can stay if you want to."

"I don't think I should. This was incredible, but like I said, what we just did is all I want. We're not really dating, right?"

He frowned. "You made it very clear you don't like mushy feelings to be involved."

"Mushy?"

He shrugged.

"You really are a romantic, aren't you?"

"I can be."

"Well, there's no need to seduce me with talk of mushy feelings. I'm easy."

"Sean, I—"

"I should go." If I stayed, my heart was in danger. I didn't mind leaving with a sore ass or a sore throat, but I needed my heart to be whole. I slid from the bed and reached for my pants, wishing my hands weren't shaking.

Blake took hold of my arm before I could pull them on. "Look at me, Sean."

I drew in a breath to steady myself first.

"Are you all right?"

"I'm fine. I just need to be on my own. This was very cathartic, but I can't process it while I'm with you."

He grinned. "Nice word."

"I know big words. I'm not as vapid as I pretend to be."

"I was teasing. I've never thought of you as vapid."

"You see too much." And that scared me more than anything.

Blake left the room while I dressed, and when I walked into the kitchen he had a bottle of water for me along with a Tupperware full of leftovers. "I wish you'd let me make you some tea."

"I'll make some at home."

"Do you have something soothing?"

I thought about that. Avery made tea sometimes, but I never really paid attention to what kind. "I'm not sure."

He reached into the cabinet and handed me a packet. "Take this then."

I wished I could let myself stay. Blake would take care of me, be like the Daddy I pretended not to want, but that was too much. "Thanks."

"I'll call you in a few days, okay?"

"Okay. Thank you. For all of this."

He smiled. "You're welcome. I like giving you what you need."

Heat rushed to my face, and I hurried out the door.

10

BLAKE

I WAITED until Wednesday to call Sean. I wanted to give him some space and time to practice being good.

"Hi, Blake."

"Hi, Sean. Have you been a good boy this week?"

He laughed nervously. "Um… kind of."

"It's a yes or no question."

"Yes, mostly."

"Confess."

His sharp intake of breath sounded more turned on than shocked. He liked having me do this.

"I was late to work this morning. I kept hitting snooze."

That was easy enough to fix. "Don't use snooze anymore. Is that clear?"

"Not even once?"

"Sean."

"Sorry, sir." He sounded more contrite than he usually did when corrected.

"I want you to forget it's even an option."

"Yes, sir."

I heard someone snickering in the background.

"Sorry, that's my asshole roommate."

"I'll tell you everything he's done," Avery shouted.

Oh, this could get good. "What would he tell me you've done this week?"

"Nothing? Nothing at all." Sean was trying way too hard to convince me of that.

"Hand him the phone."

"No. That's a terrible idea. He'll—Avery! What are you—"

"Hi, Blake."

"Did you need to tell me something?" I asked.

"Yes!" There were muffled noises and then Avery shouting "Sean! Stop it!" before he started laughing so hard I couldn't understand him.

"Is Sean tickling you?"

"Yes. Help!"

"Put me on speaker."

More noises of struggling and then, "Speaker's on."

"Sean, sit down and let me talk to Avery."

"Not fair. You two can't gang up on me." His voice was too muffled for me to tell if he was annoyed or upset.

"Is he actually mad?" My stomach clenched at the thought. I hoped I hadn't misread this situation.

"No, he's pouting. It's so adorable. I wish you could see him."

I laughed. "I wish I could too."

"Don't listen to him," Sean said. "He's evil."

"You're evil," Avery said. "You trashed the bathroom and used my makeup, and you were late this morning because you were still up watching some reality show at two a.m."

"I couldn't sleep." I could hear the pout in Sean's voice.

"You couldn't stop watching that contestant's fine ass."

"Thank you, Avery," I said, trying not to laugh. "Give the phone back to Sean now."

I heard some murmurs and "wait until I see Graham

again" from Sean. The background noise lessened, and Sean said, "I'm in trouble, aren't I?"

"You are."

"What are you going to do to me?" Oh, that whiny voice. He really needed a good spanking.

"Keep you wondering, imagining what punishments I'll come up with. Maybe then you'll remember to behave for the rest of the week."

"I'm sorry, sir."

"You should be." I quickly double-checked my calendar. "I have an event I need to work on Friday. So why don't you come over Saturday afternoon."

"Okay."

"Be there at three o'clock, and bring a change of clothes, comfy ones."

"You want me to stay?"

I hated how panicked he sounded at the thought. "I do, but I won't push you. That's not what the clothes are for. I have a surprise for you."

"Can't you at least give me a hint about it?"

"Sean."

He sighed. "Sorry, sir."

"Good night, boy."

"Good night."

"Whoa, what is that?" Sean asked.

As soon as he'd arrived at my condo, I'd led him into my office where I'd laid out all the toys we would use today.

"This?" I held up the ominous-looking metal object so he could see it better. "It's an anal speculum."

"Whoa. You're serious going to put that in my ass?"

"If you allow me to. I remember how much you enjoyed holding yourself open for me."

Sean scowled. "I'm not sure 'enjoy' is the right word."

I reached for his cock, which was straining against his tight jeans. "You're hard just thinking about it."

He just kept scowling, so I squeezed his cock and he jumped.

"Brat. It embarrassed you, and that turned you on."

His cheeks turned an adorable shade of pink. If I didn't have plans for him, I'd jerk him off right there just to watch as he flushed more and more.

"A lot of things embarrass me, but they don't turn me on. Like when I write something for work, and my supervisor tells me it's crap, or when I trip and fall just walking down the street, or—"

"Would having your hole stretched open while waiting for me on your hands and knees embarrass you in the way that turns you on? You'd know that every time I looked at you while you waited, I'd see your ass on display and know what a slut you are for me."

His eyes went wide. "Holy fuck."

"I thought so. Strip, and get on all fours."

"Right here?"

"Yes. I'm going to be sitting there" —I pointed to my desk — "and getting some work done. I want you where I can see you."

"Fuck."

"That's the last time you're allowed to speak unless I ask you a question, you're acknowledging an order, or you need to use your safeword."

"Yes, sir."

"While you're on the floor waiting for me, I want you to think about all the things you've done since we talked. When

I'm ready, I'll give you a chance to confess, and then I'll spank you to remind you how important it is to be a good boy."

"Yes, Daddy."

He sucked in his breath, like he hadn't meant to say that.

"I'm here to take care of you. You understand that, right, boy?"

"Yes, sir, Daddy, sir."

He stood there, just staring at me, and I fought the urge to smile. I could feel the need rolling off him.

After a few seconds, I said, "I'm waiting."

"Oh. Right. I... I'm sorry, sir."

He was so cute when he got all flustered. When he was nervous about pleasing me, he dropped his bratty attitude, and I could tell how glad he was that I was taking him in hand. If only I could get him to soften like this when we weren't in scene space. Maybe the plans I had for later would make that happen.

Or maybe they won't, and you'll have to be happy with what he's willing to give.

Maybe so, but telling myself that didn't stop me from falling for him more each time I saw him.

Once he was naked, I grabbed my exercise mat and rolled it out for him. I intended to leave him there for a while, and I didn't want the hard floor to prevent him from obeying. This wasn't about making his knees sore; it was about teaching him patience and submission.

He sank to his knees gracefully and then positioned himself on all fours with his back arched to better display his ass. He totally knew how hot he was. I knelt behind him with lube and the speculum, but before I touched his ass, I reached under him and wrapped a hand around his cock.

"I bet I could make you come with a few strokes, and we haven't even started yet."

I slid my hand along him, and he worked his hips, trying to get more.

"So eager."

"Please!" he whined.

I slapped his ass. "Hush." As I teased his slit, his muscles went rigid. "You want to talk, don't you? I bet if you could, you'd to beg me to fuck you and plead with me not to leave you here, but all you're allowed to do is feel. You aren't going to be coming for a long time."

He whimpered when I let go, but I ignored it as I slicked up my fingers.

"I'm going to open your ass with my fingers, and then I'll slide the speculum in. I'm not going to open it very wide. It might be uncomfortable, but it shouldn't hurt, so let me know if it does."

"Okay."

I slapped his ass hard enough to leave a handprint.

"Owww. Fuck."

I did it again.

"Yes, sir. Sorry, sir."

I used two fingers to open him up, fucking him with them until he was trembling. "You want to move, don't you? You want to fuck back onto my fingers."

"Yes, sir."

"You're doing such a good job of holding still, though. You can be disciplined when you need to."

"I… yes. Thank you, sir."

I pushed in deeper and brushed his sweet spot.

He cried out and worked his hips. "That's… not… fair."

"No talking." I pressed against his prostate again.

"Fuck!"

I slapped his ass where it was still red. "I just gave you a compliment, but now you're being a very bad boy. If this keeps up, you won't get to come today."

"No. Please. I'm sorry. It's just… I'm sorry, sir."

"Shh," I said as I stroked his back. He was shaking, and I didn't want to push him too far. "I know how hard this is. I'm testing your limits, and I'm not angry that you couldn't hold still. You have to speak respectfully, though."

"Yes, sir."

I lubed up the speculum. It was time to see if he could take it. "This might be cold."

I pushed it in, and he yelped. "Wow! That's… Yes, sir."

He managed to stay still and silent as I finished inserting it, but when I started to open it, he sucked in his breath and wiggled as if trying to escape it. "Feels so strange."

"I bet it does. Tell me about it." Talking would distract him as he got used to it.

"I thought it would be like a dildo, but harder, but it's not really. It's like I should feel full but I don't. I need to be filled more than I did before. And the pressure is weird."

"Does it hurt?"

He seemed to be thinking for a moment. "No."

"Good." I spread him just a bit more and then stopped.

"Are you okay?"

"Yes, sir." His voice was shaky, but I thought he'd adjust all right.

"I'm going to get some work done while you display yourself for me. I expect you to be still and silent."

"Yes, sir."

I ran a hand down his back. "You can use your safeword any time if you need it."

"I know. Thank you, Daddy."

I loved that he was saying that more. "You're so fucking hot like this." He shivered as I traced the edge of his stretched hole. It was hard for me to walk away from him, but he needed to learn patience, and the wait would be worth it.

I forced myself to finish all the work that needed immediate attention. I'd told Sean I'd be watching him, but that was a lie. I only glanced his way occasionally to make sure he was okay. But even without looking, I still heard every shift of his body and every small sigh that escaped him. I'd been trained to be more aware of my surroundings than most people. That was a good thing for a security consultant but terrible when a man was trying to double-check a spreadsheet formula, and all he could hear was the ragged breathing of his submissive across the room.

It was only after I'd closed my laptop that I allowed myself to really take in the way his ass gaped, the slight tremble in his limbs, the hard length of his cock jutting between his legs. All of it was for me. He was waiting, needing, and I wanted to pull the speculum out and fuck him right there on the floor, but that wasn't what I had planned. I wondered if he knew it was just as difficult for me to wait as it was for him.

I walked across the room, forcing myself to move slowly. "You make a very nice display."

"Thank you, sir."

"It's time to take the speculum out now." I knelt behind him, collapsed the device, and pulled it from his ass. He managed to hold still as I did so. I thought he deserved a small reward, though he might see it as a punishment, since he wouldn't be allowed to come. "You feel empty, don't you?"

"Yes, sir."

"You want something to fill your ass?"

"Yes, please, sir."

I slicked up my fingers and pressed at his hole with three of them. "Push back, and take them all the way in."

He obeyed immediately, and when the digits were buried in him, he sighed. "Thank you, sir."

"Ride them."

He did, working his whole body back and forth, swallowing my fingers, even taking my pinky too. His breaths grew more and more ragged.

"Please, Daddy," he begged. "Please. Can I come?"

"No." I pulled my fingers from his ass. "You're not allowed to come until after we've played a game."

"A game?"

"Yes." I wiped my hand on a towel I'd laid beside him and stood. "Sit back slowly and stand when you're ready. It's okay if you need a moment; I don't want you to be dizzy."

When he was on his feet, I took both his hands and turned him to face me. "You're doing so good today. I'm going to put the bridle on you and restrain your hands behind your back. Then I'm going to lead you around and give you commands."

"Commands? Like I'm a pony?"

I nodded.

"What happens if I can't follow them, sir?"

"I'll use the crop on you."

He shivered. "Do I get to wear the tail plug?"

I shook my head. "You haven't earned the tail plug yet. You'll get there, though. I'm proud of how far you've already come."

"I loved sucking your cock, sir."

I smiled. "I could tell. I enjoyed your enthusiasm."

"Thank you, sir."

"I'm going to put the bridle on you, and this time I'm going to use the bit, so you won't be able to talk. I'll give you the ball you used before, and you can drop it if you need to stop, okay?"

"Yes, sir."

I attended to all the straps, making sure the bridle was secure. "Open your mouth." He did, and I fit the bit in and clipped it on the other side of his face. Unlike a metal bit used on a horse, this one was made of fabric and wouldn't hurt him.

"Nod if that feels okay."

He did. "Good. Now put your hands behind your back."

I placed cuffs around his wrists and then clipped the cuffs together. "Nod if your wrists feel okay."

He did. "Good boy." I put the ball in his hand and then attached a lead rope to his bridle. "We're going to get started. I expect you to do as I say. If you're having trouble, I'll help you, but if you deliberately disobey, I have the crop." I picked it up and slapped it against my hand, which made him jump. "Follow me."

11

SEAN

It FELT weird to have the bit in my mouth. I'd never let a partner gag me before, but I trusted Blake. And I had the ball in my hand in case I needed to tell him to stop.

I walked behind him into the living room, but it was hard to stay balanced with my hands behind my back, especially when I was distracted by the throb of my cock and the way my ass felt so empty after having the speculum in.

Blake had cleared away most of the furniture from the living room. I hadn't even noticed when he'd let me in. Talk about thinking with your dick.

"Trot," Blake ordered. I hadn't expected him to start so abruptly, but I managed to obey, keeping up with his long strides as he led me around the room.

"Walk," he commanded a few seconds later. I slowed, and he patted my "flank." "Good boy. Now circle around."

He used the rope to guide me in a small circle. This wasn't hard, and it was nice to know all I had to do was follow what he said.

"Trot." I picked up my pace. We went around the room and started again.

"Whoa!"

I tried to stop too quickly, and I lost my balance, stumbling forward. He grabbed my arm and then gave me a light swat on the ass. "Pay attention to your balance."

I tried to respond, forgetting about the bit. That earned me another swat. My ass stung, but I liked knowing Blake would correct me, even if I didn't want to think too much about why I felt that way.

"You're to stay right here while I set up some jumps."

Jumps? I was worried I wouldn't be able to do what he asked, but as I watched, he laid out a few rolled-up blankets and a small stool. That, I could handle.

He took the lead rope in his hand again and started moving. "Walk on."

I followed him. "We're going through the jumps. I expect you to clear each one and keep your balance."

I did the jumps easily, but then he had me do them at a trot and then a canter. I wasn't really sure what cantering was, but I got the idea that it was faster than trotting but not full-out running. I stumbled going over the stool and nearly fell. He swatted my ass hard enough to make me yelp this time.

"You have to concentrate, not just run."

I wanted to tell him to fuck off, but I just nodded like a good ponyboy.

"We're going to play a game now. It's like Simon Says. I'll give commands, but if I don't say 'Trainer says' before the command, you ignore it. Do you understand?"

I nodded.

"Whenever you mess up, I'll crop your ass or thighs."

I nodded again and drew in a shaky breath. I could do this. It wasn't hard; I just had to concentrate.

I did well at first. But then the commands came faster.

"Trainer says canter. Trainer says walk. Trainer says jump. Jump again."

I jumped, and he slapped my thigh. I missed the next command, and he cropped me again.

The more I messed up, the harder it was to concentrate until I was missing almost everything. After one last stroke to my ass, Blake said, "That's enough."

I sighed in relief. My ass and thighs stung, the bit was bothering me, and my cock was so fucking hard.

He took off my bridle and uncuffed my hands. After he'd massaged my wrists, he said, "Go lie on your stomach on the bed."

"What are you going to do, sir?" As soon as I spoke, I realized I'd broken the rules again. "I'm sorry. I didn't mean…"

"I'm going to spank you, and I'm adding five strokes for that."

I felt the sting of tears behind my eyes. I thought him using the crop while we played and making me wait before was my punishment.

He stroked my cheeks. "It's okay, Sean. I'm doing this because I care for you. You need this. You need to be spanked for all you've done this week. Do you understand?"

"I thought this was my punishment."

He smiled. "No, this was a game. I will spank you every time we're together, separate of any game or other challenges I set for you. You need that."

Did I? My ass already stung, but there was something about a spanking that was different.

"I… I want to be good."

"You are. I'm proud of you."

"But you still want to punish me." I usually loved being spanked, so I wasn't sure why this was so hard for me today.

"I need to punish you, and you need that release. Once I'm finished, I'm going to fuck you."

"You are?"

"Yes."

I could do this. I could take more if I was finally going to get his cock. "Thank you, sir."

I got into position on the bed, and a few moments later, I heard him enter the room.

He didn't give me any warning, he just brought his hand down hard on my ass. He kept going, spanking me again and again until my ass felt like it was on fire. I tried to stay still, but I couldn't help shifting my hips against the bed. His hand hurt, but it also made me crazy with the need to come. I had to get some friction on my cock.

"Five more. These are the ones you earned by talking when you shouldn't."

I wasn't sure I could take more, not without coming. "Please, sir."

He ignored me, slapping my ass hard. I cried out from pain and want, and I thrust against the bed, no longer trying to hide what I was doing. I wanted to be good, wanted to please him, but I couldn't stop. I needed more. I needed... "Fuck!" My climax slammed through me, and I rutted against the bed as I spilled my seed.

The spanking ended, and he didn't say anything until my body stilled.

"Look at me, boy."

I rose on my elbows and turned to face him, dreading the disappointment I was sure to see. "I'm sorry, Daddy." I needed to use that word, needed him to be that for me.

"I'm sure you are, boy. We'll deal with this after I fuck you. Turn over and hold your legs up."

I did, and I watched as he rolled on a condom and slicked himself up. When he pushed in, I was glad I'd been wearing a plug. He didn't go slow, not that I wanted it to be. I wanted to be fucked hard and deep with no mercy, and he gave me exactly that.

He took my cock in his hand and worked me at the same pace as his thrusts. Was he going to let me come again? Because I was already most of the way there.

"Blake. Fuck. That's… I need you."

He smiled at me, obviously loving how desperate I was. "Come for me, Sean. Don't hold anything back."

"Thank you. Oh, fuck. Thank you."

He worked me faster and faster, until my back bowed and I cried out, shooting across my torso.

He slowed his pace while I rode out my orgasm. When I was done, he ran his fingers through my cum and held them up to me. I sucked them as thoroughly as I would have his cock, which seemed to drive him crazy. He thrust into me a few more times and then with a rough shout, he pumped out his release, holding my gaze the whole time.

When I was capable of thought again, Blake was lying on his side, watching me. He reached out and ran his fingers over my sweaty chest. Then he took my hand and kissed my palm. Warmth spread over me, not the heat that had consumed me as he'd fucked me, but a feeling that was way too intense. One that made me think of words I'd sworn never to say to a man.

"You're not allowed to come until I see you again."

"Wait. What?" I'd been thinking how frighteningly romantic this all was, and now he was telling me I wasn't allowed to get off for like a week.

"No orgasms until you're with me again. That's your punishment for coming without permission."

"But I—"

"I can make you wait longer. I don't have to let you come next time you're here."

"No, please. I'll be good."

He kissed my hand again. "I hope so. Do you have to leave now?"

"I don't have any plans or anything, but—"

"Then stay, because I have something I want to show you."

Was I brave enough to do that? "All right. I'll stay for whatever this surprise is."

"You're welcome to stay all night. I'd like that."

"But you won't let me come again if I do?"

He raised his brows. "You just came twice. How insatiable are you?"

"Around you? Very."

He rolled on top of me and pinned my wrists. "It's going to take a long time to teach you discipline."

"Promise me you'll keep trying?"

"Right now?"

"Um… maybe not now."

He chuckled. "I have so many plans for you." He kissed me, and I opened for him, letting him thoroughly fuck my mouth with his tongue as I worked my quickly thickening cock against his. Without warning, he sat back. "But right now, it's time for a shower."

I stared at him, panting. How had he made me want him again when my ass ached and I should be drained?

"Come on." He held out his hand, and I took it.

We showered and dressed with minimal groping, though the sight of him in loose gray sweats could easily have sent me to my knees.

"Are you ready to go?"

"Go? We're leaving the apartment?"

He smiled. "Yes. We're going to watch the sunset from the roof. Should I bring a bottle of wine, since we're done with our scene for tonight?"

"That sounds great. I'd actually love to find out what

86

you're like after a few drinks."

"It will take more than a few. I was in the Navy, remember?"

I rolled my eyes. "Navy SEAL prowess wins again."

"Are you hungry?"

I considered that for a moment. "Yeah. You gave me quite a workout."

"I sure did. I've got some cheese and fruit or maybe—"

"I usually eat chips and ice cream when I drink with Avery."

He winced. "Ice cream would not go with this wine."

"Avery and I usually hit the vodka, but you're a lot more civilized."

"Apparently." He zipped the insulated cooler he'd been packing. "We have cheese, grapes, wheat crackers, and a nice bottle of wine, which I think you'll appreciate if you give it a chance."

"No swigging from the bottle then?"

He rolled his eyes. "No."

"Where did you learn to be so grown up?"

"I just like nice things. It's the gayest thing about me."

I grinned. "Except the fact that you like to bury your dick in my ass."

"Yes, except for that." We laughed as he led me to the stairs.

"You're not completely butch," I said as I thought more about it. "You do have nice clothes, and—" We stepped out onto the roof, and the view nearly took my breath. I could see across the city to the mountain ranges beyond. "Holy shit, it's gorgeous up here."

"It's awesome, isn't it?"

"Yeah. Wow." We walked toward a fire pit that was surrounded by some chairs and a few small tables. "Are these yours?"

"I bought some of them, but all the tenants share the stuff up here."

"This is really amazing. Thank you for bringing me up here."

"You're welcome." His voice was softer than usual, and while I loved the demanding Dom side of him, I liked this too. A lot.

"Sit down." I gestured toward a wicker sofa with thick cushions. "I'll set this up for us."

He frowned. "I can do that."

"No, I want to."

"All right."

I kept glancing at him as I sliced cheese and laid it on a plate with crackers and grapes. He looked like a lounging jungle cat, who'd come to rest after a day of prowling the trees. His legs were spread, and he had one arm on the side of the couch and the other stretched across the back as he gazed out at the mountains.

When he turned to look at me, his lips quirked up. "Like what you see?"

"So very much." I wanted to crawl between his legs and suck him off. "Have you ever fucked someone up here?"

His eyes widened. "No."

"There's always a first time."

He shook his head. "Open the wine, Sean."

"I could make it worth the risk."

"I'm sure you could, but I want to watch the sunset with you."

I tried one more tactic. "I could suck you off really quickly."

"No, I like to savor you."

"You have an answer for everything, don't you?" I said as I wrestled with the cork.

"I do. Give me that."

He took the wine from me and had the cork out in less than a second. "How did you do that? It was stuck."

"I'm a SEAL."

"So you can do anything?"

He shrugged. "Pretty much."

I narrowed my eyes. "When you do that—hide behind the 'I'm a SEAL' answer—it's a defense, isn't it? Like me being bratty."

His eyes widened, and I was afraid I'd gone too far. "Oh, shit. Was that wrong to say?"

"No. You just surprised me, and I don't exactly like how right you are."

I smiled as I poured his wine. "You don't have to pretend with me. I already know you're fucking amazing."

He frowned. "I was just teasing."

"I know, but I wanted to say that anyway."

"Thank you." He took my hand and something in my chest hurt; I was terribly afraid it was the walls I'd built around my heart crumbling.

I handed him the glass of wine and joined him on the couch. "Have you ever had anyone take care of you?"

"That's not—"

He looked up, and it was like he was seeing into me again, but this time, I might have been seeing into him as well. "Blake, please tell me."

"No, not in a long time, not in the way you probably mean it, at least. I didn't have a very good childhood. My parents died when I was six. They took care of me. They loved me deeply, but I only have a few memories of them. My aunt and uncle adopted me, but they only did what they had to. They weren't cruel or anything, but they hadn't meant to have kids, and it was obvious I was a duty, not a joy. I did well in school, and they used their connections to help me get into the naval academy. After I graduated, I did SEAL training, and my team cared for me. I knew they would die for me like I would for them, but I was the platoon leader, and… well…"

"You were the one who took care of them. The one they relied on."

He nodded. "And now?"

"Now I'm… It's hard not to have a team anymore. I still talk to all the guys, and I try to see them a few times a year, but it's not easy to make our schedules mesh."

I laid my hand on his thigh. "I'm sorry. Have you made many friends here?"

"Not really, not outside work."

"Maybe I could help you with that?"

"You want to do that?"

I frowned at him. "Of course I do. This doesn't have to be all about you taking care of me. We could go out with Avery and Graham sometime."

"Like a double date?"

Heat rushed to my face. No wonder he was surprised. I'd told him this was supposed to be just sex and kinky shit, but… "Yeah, like that."

He gave me a huge smile. "I'd love that."

"I'll talk to Avery and let you know when Graham will be here again."

After that, we watched the sunset in silence. As it grew dark, the wind picked up. Blake wrapped an arm around me, and I snuggled close. He was warm and cozy, and I felt more at ease with him than anybody, maybe even Avery. That should scare the hell out of me, but in that moment I chose to let it be okay.

Eventually, I was shivering like crazy, even with Blake holding me.

"Time to go back in?" he asked.

I nodded.

We packed up our stuff and headed downstairs. When we were back in his condo, he asked if I wanted to stay and watch a movie.

Things were already moving to a place I wasn't sure I wanted to be. I was about to say no, but he spoke first. "We'll watch whatever you choose."

"Really?"

"Yes."

"So you'd watch *Tangled* with me?"

"I told you I liked Disney, and who can resist Flynn Rider?"

I grinned. "Yeah, I know, and Rapunzel is so awesome with that hair and the frying pan."

"Even if it wasn't one of my favorites too, I would watch it with you because I like doing things that make you happy."

He was serious. I was sure of it. I was also sure he'd been serious when he'd said that our time together was about more than making me come, or preventing me from it. He was teaching me things about myself, things I'd been afraid to think about. That was scary, but also exhilarating.

"I want to be as good for you as you are for me."

He squeezed my hand. "You are."

"No, that's not true. I—"

"Sean?"

"Yes?

"Shut up and just watch the movie with me."

"All right." I bounded over the back of the sofa and landed beside him. "Ha. You haven't tamed me yet."

He frowned. "I don't want to tame you."

"You want to free me, I know." I hadn't understood that when he'd said it, but now…

"Do you? Do you really?"

"I think I'm starting to."

"Good."

12

BLAKE

SEAN RAN down the sidewalk toward me. When he came to a stop, inches away, he glanced at his watch and then pumped his fist in the air. "I'm not late."

I couldn't help but smile. "No, you're not." We were standing outside of his and Avery's favorite restaurant. Sean had visited his mother the previous weekend, and we'd only been able to spend one evening together this week. I'd missed him. He pulled me into his arms and kissed me. I growled when he nipped at my lower lip as he pulled away, but he just gave me a cheeky grin.

"The next step is for you to learn to be on time without racing to get somewhere."

He sighed dramatically. "You'll never be satisfied, will you?"

I grabbed his hips and pulled him against me. "You better satisfy me later tonight if you want any satisfaction yourself."

"I'll satisfy you more than once, Daddy."

"My slutty boy."

A whistle had Sean pulling back. I'd seen Graham and Avery approaching. But I hadn't wanted to let Sean go.

"Hi, Blake," Avery said. "Let me know if you need any information about Sean's behavior this week."

"Avery." Graham glared at him.

"After all the teasing I've put up with from Sean, don't you think he deserves it?" Avery huffed when Graham's expression didn't change. Someone was getting a spanking tonight —or worse.

Sean was giving Avery a death glare.

"Don't look at me like that when I made you look so good tonight."

I took more time to appreciate Sean's subtle makeup and well-styled hair. "You did an amazing job."

Avery beamed. "Thank you."

"I should book an appointment with you soon."

He studied me for a moment. "I know exactly what I'd do with your hair. I don't suppose you'd want a makeover too?"

I glanced at Sean, and his eyes were wide. "You like that idea? Seeing me in makeup?"

"Fuck, yes. It would be so unexpected and totally hot."

I looked back at Avery and smiled. "We'll see."

Lucky, Avery mouthed to Sean.

"Hey!" Graham protested.

Avery rubbed his arm soothingly. "You know I like you just as you are."

"I told you I'd let you make me over if you really wanted to."

Avery and Sean both shook their heads.

"It's just not your look," Avery said. "I get to do your hair and shop for suits with you. That's all I need."

"All?" Graham arched his brows.

"Um… I didn't mean…"

Graham was looking at Avery like he wanted to devour him.

I cleared my throat. "Before we risk any public indecency charges, let's go inside."

The hostess showed up to our table, and Sean insisted I try a blood orange margarita. I was not going to say no to that. The rest of the table had the same, and Graham ordered us some lobster nachos as an appetizer.

"Be sure to save room for churros," Avery said.

"Sean's already warned me."

"And Mexican hot chocolate," Sean said. He and Avery looked like they might swoon. I started to wonder if I'd gotten in over my head having dinner with both of them.

"The churros really are amazing," Graham assured me. "So is the filet. It's prepared a little differently every time I come, but always cooked perfectly."

"Thanks. I know what I'm ordering."

When the waitress returned with our drinks, Sean ordered grilled scallops. The rest of us got the fillet, and we chose a large apple and feta salad to share.

When our waitress headed toward the kitchen, Avery said, "We've got some big news." I could feel Sean tense beside me as Avery looked my way. "Did Sean tell you Graham and I found a house we wanted to buy?"

"He did."

"Our offer has been accepted."

"Really?" Sean asked.

"Yes, we close in a week and a half. Or really, Graham does."

"It's our house," Graham said in a don't-fuck-with-me voice.

Sean sputtered. "A week and half? I thought buying a house took ages." The last word came out as a squeak.

"I'm paying cash. That speeds things up."

Sean was obviously a bit freaked out about how soon he'd be losing Avery. I took his hand under the table and squeezed it as I redirected the conversation. "Graham, you live in Charlotte now, right?"

"That's right. I'm moving up here to be with my boy all the time."

Avery grinned and leaned over for a kiss.

"Are you going to be looking for a new roommate?" I asked Sean.

"Yes. One that won't rat me out all the time."

Avery stuck his tongue out, and Sean flipped him off. I ignored their antics though, because what if... No, Sean and I weren't ready for that yet, were we? He could barely stay the night with me without getting antsy to leave. No way in hell could he live with me, no matter how awesome it would be. I wouldn't need anyone to tell on him then. I'd know all his transgressions and exactly how to punish and reward him.

"Blake?"

Shit, had Sean been talking to me?

"Sorry, I got lost in thought there. I was making a mental list of punishments, since I'm sure I'll need more when Avery's not there to encourage you."

Sean rolled his eyes. "My new roommate will probably fuss at me every time I leave something on the floor just like Avery does."

"Possibly," Avery said. "But he won't be me."

"That's for damn sure," Sean replied.

I looked over at Graham, who was watching Avery with a smile on his face. "Are they always like this?"

"Yes," he said without any hesitation.

"So where's the house you're buying?"

"It's in West Asheville off Brevard Road."

"Wow. That's such an awesome area. One of the guys who works for me lives on Brevard in a duplex."

"You live downtown?" Graham asked.

"A little north of downtown, but close."

"His condo is amazing," Sean interjected. "You can see everything from the roof."

His enthusiasm warmed me.

"How'd you find such a great place?" Avery asked.

"A guy I knew from the Navy used to live there and gave me the tip. The owner gives a military discount, so my rent isn't much higher than the other places I was looking at that were miles out of town."

"Is most of your work in Asheville?" Graham asked.

"We do security for some events here and consult with businesses like Thrust, but I also do consulting for companies all over the region."

"Do you do consultation for apartment complexes?"

I nodded as I took a sip of my margarita, which was every bit as good as Sean had promised. "I do. I've worked with several complexes here."

"I'll keep that in mind," Graham said. "I've put in an offer on a few complexes in Charlotte that are in need of remodeling. If I end up buying them, I'll have you take a look. It's a transitional area, and I know safety is going to be a top concern for the clientele I hope to attract."

"Enough business," Avery said.

Graham raised a brow and stared at him.

"Please."

I pulled a card from my wallet and handed it to Graham. "Call me anytime." Then, looking at Avery, I said, "Tell me more about your new house."

"It's amazing. I've loved it ever since I saw it when I was going to a friend's house years ago. It's foursquare style and has a wrap-around porch, which is just perfect. And it's this deep blue that I love."

Graham smiled. "It really is a perfect house."

"It sounds great. I love the older houses in that area."

Avery kept going, giving more details about the house,

but I wasn't listening carefully, because I was watching the interplay between him and Graham. Occasionally, Graham would jump in and finish one of Avery's sentences. Avery would smile at him, and it was so obvious how in love they were.

I glanced over at Sean and saw that he was watching them too. If he could look at them with such longing, did that mean we could... No, I was getting ahead of myself.

A few seconds later, Sean's gaze met mine. He must have realized I knew what he was doing, because he sank his teeth into his lower lip and got very interested in his drink.

The waitress brought our nachos then, and we all dug in. They were as amazing as they sounded.

After taking a sip of his drink, Avery said, "I'm very impressed with what you've done with Sean." The grunt he made then likely meant Sean had kicked him under the table.

"Thank you. I'm trying."

Avery nodded. "Believe me. I know how hard you have it."

"I'm sitting right here," Sean protested.

I leaned over and kissed his cheek. "And looking amazing doing so."

He just glared at me.

"How long have you two been roommates?" I asked.

"Forever," Avery said.

Sean rolled his eyes. "Five years. That's right, isn't it?"

Avery nodded. "And that's way long enough for me to know all his bad habits."

I grinned at him. "We should have coffee sometime."

"Graham, would you like to move to the bar?" Sean asked.

The server proved she had impeccable timing by showing up right then with our entrees. We all became too enraptured by our food to deliver any more snark. After I'd savored several bites, I looked over at Sean. He was watching me with heat in his eyes.

"Like what you see?" I asked.

"I do." He glanced toward the back of the restaurant. "I wonder if anyone is in the bathroom."

"What did I tell you?"

"You said no club bathrooms. This place is classy."

"No public bathroom sex period."

He stuck out his lower lip in an adorable pout before turning his attention back to his food.

Dinner was fantastic, both the food and the company. For dessert, we all ordered churros which came with hot chocolate, and at Avery's suggestion, we had shots of Bailey's added.

As soon as our plates were set on the table, Sean dipped a churro into the caramel sauce and held it up to me. "Taste."

I bit into it and groaned. It tasted like magic. Sean held my gaze as I chewed and made noises much like those he usually heard during sex.

Avery coughed. "You two need to take that to a room." But his protest died when Graham held a churro up for him.

After a little more teasing, we each ate our own desserts. I couldn't believe I'd never eaten at this place. I was already planning a time to bring Sean back.

After we settled up, we all hugged goodbye and promised to get together again soon. Sean and I were so full of good food, we were both content to snuggle on the couch. We ended up watching *Thor: Ragnarok* and *Lady and the Tramp*, an odd combo, but they both made Sean smile. Late that night, we jerked each other off in the shower, then tumbled into bed.

"I guess I really can't pretend this is just about you teaching me to submit anymore," Sean said, as I pulled him against me. His voice was low, and I could tell how nervous he was.

"You relaxing and letting go like this, being comfortable here with me, that's a form of submission too."

"It feels so good, much better than I thought it would."

As he drifted to sleep, I allowed myself to imagine him moving in with me. I had a good life, but if Sean were here like this every day, it would be perfect.

13

SEAN

I DIDN'T GO home until early afternoon the next day. Blake had cooked me a delicious brunch, and then I'd kissed him goodbye, which led to me being pinned against the wall. Then we were naked, and I was on my knees. Things went as expected from there.

When I opened the door, Avery was sitting on the couch typing on his iPad. "Hello, Mr. I-Never-Used-to-Stay-The-Night."

I flipped him off.

"You seem to do a lot of things with Blake that are on your 'never do' list. Did I hear you call him Daddy when we walked up last night?"

I sighed. "Fine. You were totally right. The Daddy thing is hot."

Avery grinned. "It sure as shit is."

I waited for him to say more, but he didn't. "So that's it? You're not going to make fun of me?"

Avery tapped the cushion beside him. "Come sit."

"Uh-oh. This is an it's-time-to-get-serious talk, isn't it?"

He nodded. "Am I going to have to break out the vodka to get you to open up like last time?"

"It's one-thirty in the afternoon."

"When has that ever stopped you?"

"Fair point. And I need to talk to someone. It might as well be you."

"It damn well should be me, and if we need vodka, I'll get it."

I flopped down next to him. "I'm going to miss you."

He wrapped an arm around me, and I laid my head on his shoulder. "I'll be right across town."

"I know, but it won't be the same."

Avery pressed his head against mine. "No, it won't. I'm going to miss you too."

"And you're worried about me."

"Not as much as I was."

He made me sit up, and he shifted position so we were facing each other.

"Because of Blake?"

"Partly, but also because you decided to try harder. You wouldn't be listening to Blake if you didn't want to."

"That's true."

"So, where is this going?"

"I think I'm in love with him, and I'm scared as fuck." Shit. Had I really said that? My heart was beating way too fast, and I felt like I might pass out.

"God, Sean, are you okay?"

"I... I don't know."

"Lay down. You look like a ghost."

I wanted to protest, but I also didn't want to faint, so I lay back against the arm of the couch. Avery took hold of my legs and encouraged me to move them up onto the cushions.

"Better?"

"A little." The room wasn't spinning quite as fast.

"I'm going to get you some water. I'll be right back."

I was only able to take a few sips of the water he brought. My stomach was too uneasy for more. What I really wanted to do was splash the water on my face, which felt like it was on fire.

"I didn't mean for this to happen," I told Avery as I lay down again. "I told Blake I didn't want to date, that I only wanted to have scenes like we would at the club."

"But you're the one that asked me and Graham to go out with you two."

I blew out a long breath. "I know, and I let Blake take me up on the roof of his building. We had a fucking picnic up there. He even brought a fancy bottle of wine."

Avery smiled. "Does he know how you feel?"

"I hope not."

"After seeing how he looked at you last night, I'm pretty damn sure he's in love with you too."

I groaned. "That just makes it worse."

"No, it makes it better. You're both feeling this. You should talk to him."

"What? No, I can't do that!" I wondered if you could faint while lying down.

"Blake isn't an asshole like your father."

"Avery, don't go there."

He snarled. "Someone has to. But if you won't listen to me, I could always call Felicity."

I stared at him wide-eyed. Felicity was like a force of nature. "You wouldn't. That's worse than bringing up my dad."

"I'll do what's necessary to keep you from giving up on Blake. He's good for you."

"I didn't say I was going to quit seeing him."

"Eventually, you'll either have to admit you want more or let him go so he can make a connection with someone else."

Thinking about Blake with someone else made me feel even sicker. "Can we please not talk about this anymore?"

Avery sighed. "I'll drop it for now, but the serious discussion isn't over yet."

"Oh, fuck. What else is there?"

"You need to start looking for a roommate."

I shook my head, which only made me dizzy again. "I can't do that yet."

"Why not?"

"I'm still in denial about you leaving."

"Is that going to help you pay the rent?"

"Fuck no. What about Graham's son Wren? He graduated, right? What's he doing now? Does he need an apartment?"

"He decided last minute to do the master's in architecture program at UNC-Charlotte, remember? He got in, but he wasn't sure. Then he changed his mind and decided to go."

"Oh, yeah. That's right. Have you got any other ideas?"

"I do." Avery's sly smile made me uneasy.

"Who?"

"Blake."

I was glad I hadn't just taken a sip of water. "What? I just told you—"

"I know it would be a huge step, but I bet you've already thought about it, haven't you?" He studied me closely.

How the fuck did he always know things like that? "No. Why would I?"

"Because you know how awesome it would be to have him with you all the time. You could use a full-time Daddy."

I grimaced. "That sounds so wrong."

"And yet so right?" Avery was definitely evil. Pure evil.

He laid a hand on my arm. "Just think about it, okay? And if you're really not going to ask him, start looking. We close on the house really soon, and the lease for this place has to be renewed shortly after that."

"I can take care of the rent for a month or two on my own."

"Sure you can, but if you don't find someone right away, you'll just keep putting it off and get yourself in trouble. And if you sign the lease, you're stuck here for another year."

"How do you know Blake would even want to live with me?"

Avery's knowing smile pissed me off. "I saw his face when we mentioned roommates. It was obvious what he wanted."

I frowned, not convinced. "It's a miracle that you put up with me. If Blake had to live with me, he'd be over me in no time."

Avery slid from the coffee table and knelt beside me. "Sean, I like to tease you, but I think you're an awesome person, and Blake does too."

He pulled me into his arms and held me tight. When we finally let go of each other, we both had to wipe away tears.

"I think it's time for vodka now."

Avery nodded. "Me too."

I sat up, and Avery hovered to make sure I was steady. "Better?"

"Yeah, I'll be all right."

"Promise me you'll think about talking to Blake. Even if moving in is too much, talk to him about how you feel. At the very least, don't run from this."

I wanted to protest, to tell him no way in hell would I run from the best thing that's happened to me, but Avery knew me better than that. "I don't want to hurt him."

"Telling him you love him won't do that."

How could he be sure? "I'm scared."

"I know. I'm scared about moving in with Graham. What if he can't stand being around me that much?"

"You two are so in love. He's going to keep you naked and under him—or under his belt—all day long. I'd be more worried you won't have time for anything but sex than worried he'll get tired of you."

Avery glared at me.

"Seriously, Avery, that man is crazy about you."

"And Blake is—"

I held up my hand. "Vodka. I need vodka."

14

SEAN

A FEW DAYS LATER, I was already missing Blake—*see how nice it would be to live with him*—so I texted to see if he was home.

His response: *I was just thinking about calling you.*

Really?

Yes.

I'll be there in like thirty minutes.

Be ready to start a scene when you arrive.

Fuck.

annoyed emoji

Yes, sir.

And bring comfy clothes again.

I sent a thumbs-up emoji and immediately started thinking of all the things he might try to surprise me with this time.

When I knocked on the door, Blake opened it almost immediately. He was wearing a form-fitting white dress shirt tucked into tight black jeans and riding boots, fucking knee-high, gorgeous riding boots. And he had a crop in his hand.

"Um… pony play?"

He nodded. "Step inside."

When I did, he shut the door and pushed me back against it. "Don't move."

I swallowed hard. "Okay. I mean yes, sir."

He drew in a deep breath as he nuzzled my neck. "You smell so good."

Before I could respond, he was unfastening my pants. He'd never been quite this aggressive with me before, but I loved it. I could barely remember how to breathe as he pulled my cock out and started working it in slow, firm strokes. I was fully hard in seconds.

He chuckled. "Like that, do you?"

"Yes, sir. So much."

He kept jacking me off. He hadn't forbidden me from coming, but he'd also never let me come without express permission. I pressed my hands to the door, afraid my legs would give. I wanted to thrust into his grip, but I was sure he intended me to stay still. He kissed and nipped and sucked at my neck and ears as he worked me relentlessly.

When he turned his attention to my mouth, he forced my lips open with his tongue and tasted me thoroughly. I kept my hands where they were, but I kissed him back; no way could I stay passive through his onslaught. My balls tightened as he increased his pace, using my precum as lube.

I was about to beg him to stop or to let me come, but he stepped back. My eyes were wide, pupils probably huge. With my dick sticking out of my open pants, I had to look like a total slut. Blake probably loved it.

"Take off your clothes. I'm going to get your bridle and tail. I have a grooming game for us today."

"Tail?"

"You were a good boy while I used you just now, so you get to have a tail while you're my ponyboy."

"Thank you, Daddy."

He smiled. "I love when you call me that, boy."

When I was naked, I knelt on the mat he'd laid out for me. He placed the bridle over my head and put the bit in place. I saw the other things he'd laid out for me: the tail, several brushes, a cock ring, and a riding crop.

"Stamp your front feet if you need to stop."

I nodded.

He pushed a lubed finger into my ass and then another one, working them in and out to open me up. Then I felt the slick tip of a plug press against me. As he pushed it into me, the tail tickled the back of my thighs, making me groan.

"You like that?"

I nodded and hummed around the bit, making a sound very unlike a horse. He slid it in all the way, and I felt the flange settle against my hole.

"I'm going to groom you thoroughly, first your body, then your mane and tail. I think you're going to love how it feels for me to brush that long hair."

Brush... that... Oh my God, every stroke of the brush would move the plug inside me. How would I survive that?

"I'm going to use the currycomb on you in just a moment, but I want to make sure every part of you is taken care of, even your big, thick cock."

I snorted and did my best imitation of a whinny.

Blake chuckled as he wrapped a washcloth around my cock and worked it up and down. I bucked, trying to thrust, and he brought the crop down on my ass.

"Ponyboys stay still while they're groomed."

Fuck. I was too worked up from him jerking me off and inserting the plug. I wasn't sure I could keep myself from coming.

When Blake finally decided I was clean enough, he held up the cock ring where I could see it. "I think my ponyboy needs some decoration."

I held my breath as he touched me, but he put the cock ring on me with minimal teasing.

"Good boy. This is the currycomb." He held it up where I could see. It looked like a rubber gadget someone would use to scrub dishes. There was a strap to slip your hand through so you could grip it and little nubs that probably helped get dust and dirt out of a horse's coat. "It should feel good."

I nodded, and he started on my back, rubbing in circles. He was right. It was nice, lightly stimulating and not at all painful, like a loofah but less scratchy. He worked his way to my ass where he used firmer pressure. Then he moved down my thighs. By the time he finished, my skin felt alive everywhere, and I was far more relaxed, though my cock hadn't softened any.

"I'm going to use a brush now. The bristles are silky, so it won't hurt either, and it's going to make you look gorgeous." He brushed my hair, tugging it, but never hurting. The attention made my scalp feel great. He made his way down my neck and along my back in slow, sensuous strokes. I had to concentrate to stay on my hands and knees, because the brush was so soothing. I wanted to sink to the floor. I felt floaty and peaceful.

When Blake lifted my tail, making the plug press against my prostate, I gasped around the bit and wriggled, trying to get away from the too-intense sensation.

He slapped my ass with the crop, and I cried out, though it was muffled.

"I expect you to hold still."

I whined, and he cropped me again.

"I'm going to brush your tail, and you're going to be a good boy while I do it."

He ran the brush down my tail and my whole body lit up. He kept stroking it until I was sweating and panting. Then he tugged on it, and I bucked.

This time, he slapped the back of my thighs with the crop. It was too much. I pulled free of his grip and started to scramble away, but he caught me.

"Whoa! I need to keep you safe, which means you have to stay right here." He shifted so he was at my side rather than behind me, but he didn't let go. "Look at me."

I did.

"Sean, are you all right?"

I nodded. I needed him so badly, and I'd panicked for a moment, unsure I could do what he wanted.

"Stomp your feet if you want me to stop."

I kept them still. My dick ached with the need to come, but I wanted to see if I could bear it for Blake.

"I'm done brushing your tail."

I started to thank him, then remembered the bit in my mouth.

"Go back to the mat."

I crawled back on my hands and knees. The humiliation of it, the fact that I was pretending to be an animal for him, only made me harder. I wanted to be able to beg for what I needed. I moved the bit around in my mouth, wishing I could spit it out.

"I'm going to use some coat conditioner on you now."

He held it up for me to see, and as far as I could tell it was just regular lotion. He squirted some on his hands and began to rub my shoulders, then my back and ass. His hands were warm and slick and soothing. I would've been able to enjoy it more if I hadn't been so desperate to come.

I wiggled my hips just a little, unable to stay completely still. I kept expecting him to crop me, but he didn't. I think he realized I was close to my breaking point.

He reached for the bottle and squeezed out more lotion. Then he took my cock in his slick hand and started jerking me off. In seconds, I was right at the edge, ready to come. Even with the ring I didn't think I could stop myself. Tears stung my eyes. I didn't want to disappoint him.

"You're so good. Such a beautiful pony."

I was struggling to breathe around the bit. I was going to come. I was—

He stopped. When he reached for the lotion, I was scared he wasn't done, but he didn't touch my cock again. He massaged my thighs, calves, and feet. I groaned as he worked his thumbs into my arches and then massaged each of my toes.

"The last thing I need to do is condition your tail. We wouldn't want it to get all tangled."

I made a choked sound and almost stamped my "hooves." I didn't know if I could take any more stimulation without losing it. Tears welled up, and I couldn't stop them from falling as he toyed with my tail, tugging on it as he slid his hands along the length. The plug pressed against my sweet spot, and I could feel my orgasm gathering. It was happening. I was going to come. Then he stopped.

"You look perfect now." His voice was so calm, like I wasn't about to fall apart. "I'm going to clean up, and I want you to stay there, so I can enjoy how pretty you look."

I wasn't about to move, because even a current of air across my dick might make me come.

Blake took his time cleaning up all the supplies. When he'd finished, my immediate need had receded enough that I could handle his touch.

He unhooked my bridle, and I worked my jaw, glad to be free of the bit.

"Here." He held out a glass of water, and I sat back on my heels so I could take it, which of course made the plug shift inside me, but I loved the way the tail swirled over my ankles. I glanced back to see how it looked.

"Would you like to see yourself?"

"Yes, sir."

He took my hand and helped me to my feet. My legs were wobbly, so he gave me a moment to get my balance before leading me to his bedroom. When I stood in front of the mirrored door on his closet, I stared at myself in shock. The tail hung down just past the backs of my knees. It was dark brown, almost the same color as my hair. "Damn, I look hot."

"Yes, you do. Would you wear the tail at Thrust some time?"

"Fuck yes, I'd love to show this off."

"Good. Now kneel and suck me."

I watched myself as I sank to my knees, shaking my ass so my tail swished.

"I'm really looking forward to having you prance around wearing that," Blake said.

That would feel amazing. My eyes met his in the mirror, and he smiled as I took hold of his cock and slid my hand up and down, watching us the whole time.

"If I'd known you'd like this mirror so much, I would've used it sooner."

I shouldn't have been so obvious. Now he'd think up with all kinds of torments that involved the mirror, like making me watch him fuck me but not letting me come. Making me sit in front of it restrained.

"Suck me, boy."

I'd distracted myself with those hot/terrible fantasies. "Sorry, sir."

My hands were resting on his thighs, but Blake took hold of my wrists and pulled them away. "Put them behind your back."

I looked toward the mirror. My hands were crossed at the wrists just above my tail. And it looked—

"So fucking hot."

I smiled, glad Blake was enjoying this.

"Open your mouth," he ordered.

He pushed inside, and I swallowed around him, humming as I did. He slid out and back in again, going all the way down this time. I sputtered around him, and he pulled back.

"Tap my leg if you need me to stop."

"Yes, sir."

He shifted slightly, making it easier for me to see the mirror. "Watch."

I couldn't have looked away if he'd ordered me to. It was so fucking obscene to see his cock disappearing into me as he fucked my mouth. He pushed in deep and held still as he ran his thumb over my throat. "I can feel my cock there. Can you see?"

He dropped his hand, and holy fuck, there was the bulge of his cock in my throat. My own dick jumped.

He pulled out slowly, and I whimpered at the loss of him.

"Turn around and get on your hands and knees. I'm going to fuck you, and you're going to watch that too."

"Yes, sir."

"Too bad I have to take this tail out. Maybe one day, I'll fuck you with it in."

"Please."

"You'd like that?" he asked.

"Yes, sir." I'd never taken two cocks in my ass before, never thought I'd want to, but I was starting to realize that for Blake, I'd do almost anything. And love it.

"Mmm. I like what a greedy slut you are."

"I'm *your* slut, sir." And I was.

"Yes, you are." He tugged on the tail, and it popped out with a wet sound.

Seconds later, he was pushing into me. I groaned, arching my back to take him deeper.

"Watch," he ordered.

We looked so good together, and I was mesmerized by the sight of his cock slipping in and out of me. I pushed back against him, unable to stay still. I'd been ready to come since a few minutes after I'd stepped in the door.

"You want to come, don't you, boy?"

"Yes, Daddy. Please!" Watching myself call him that was so hot.

He held my hips and thrust in hard, jolting me forward. I watched with wide eyes and my mouth hanging open.

"Fuck me, Daddy."

"That's right, boy. Keep watching while I fill you with my cock."

He slowed his strokes. I was squirming and struggling against his hold, nearly out of my mind with need.

"Please let me come. Please, Daddy."

He reached under me and stroked my cock, but he still didn't give his permission. When I was so close to the edge, I no longer cared about even trying to be good. He unsnapped the cock ring, tossed it away, and said, "You can come now, boy."

He jerked me off as he fucked me, and I closed my eyes, unable to watch anymore as my body lit up with sensation that threatened to break me apart. Heat surged through me, and I literally saw stars with every pulse of my cock.

Blake kept fucking me as my body wrung itself dry. Then he seized my hips hard enough to bruise and cried out his own release, which made my cock give a final jolt as if I were trying to come all over again.

Unable to hold myself up anymore, I let my head rest against the floor. When he pulled out, I slid down flat on my stomach and let myself drift.

As if from far away, the realization came to me that I was lying in a puddle of cum on his bedroom rug. I wondered if he'd be annoyed that we got that carried away, but I was way too blissed out to worry about anything right then.

15

BLAKE

MY LEGS WERE ALMOST TOO shaky to hold me when I finally stood. Sean was so gorgeous lying there all fucked out and boneless. His pert ass made me wish I was ready for round two.

He'd been amazing as he submitted to grooming and then to me fucking him. And when he called me Daddy, it felt so damn right. I'd never had that dynamic with anyone else. I'd imagined it, but I hadn't sought it out. Was there a chance Sean would agree to a true Daddy/boy relationship?

I stepped into my en suite bathroom, cleaned myself up, and wet a washcloth for Sean. He hadn't moved, so I knelt beside him. "Roll over."

It took him a moment, like he'd been almost asleep.

"I got cum on your rug."

It should bother me that I forgot to put a towel down, but it didn't. "I have a steam cleaner. It's fine."

When I'd wiped him clean, I helped him up and pulled him onto my lap. "You're amazing, boy."

His cheeks turned pink. "I... um..."

"I have a surprise for you."

He gave me his pouty face. "I'm too tired."

"This won't take any effort."

"You want me to just lay there?"

I raised my brows. "I think we've proved how challenging that is for you."

"Bastard."

"I'm going to assume you think our scene is over, because otherwise that would earn you a wicked punishment."

"Um… yes… scene over."

I chuckled. "Right. This isn't a sex surprise."

"Nothing with tails or saddles or giant dildos?"

"Would you like a saddle or giant dildo?"

"No. Maybe. I don't know. If you're going to fuck me with the tail in, we have to stretch my ass somehow."

His words nearly made me choke. "I'll keep that in mind, but all you need to do for this is put on some clothes."

He whined. "I can't move."

"Then I'll have to dress you."

"You'd do that?"

Instead of answering, I went looking for the bag he'd brought and remembered he'd dropped it by the front door when I'd pushed him against it.

Sean was curled on his side on the floor when I got back. I really had worn him out. I dressed first, pulling on some sweats and a t-shirt. Then I knelt beside him and placed his feet in the leg holes of his shorts. I slid them up, and he lifted his hips so I could maneuver them over his ass.

"You want me commando?" he asked.

"You won't be in these clothes for long."

"I knew it was a sex surprise."

I rolled my eyes. "It's really not."

"Is that actually a thing?"

"A sex surprise?"

"No, commando. Do you special forces guys really not like to wear underwear?"

I laughed. "Sometimes. If you're deployed where it's excessively hot, you're less likely to end up with crotch rot that way."

"Oh my God, I so wish I hadn't asked." His horrified expression made me laugh.

"Other times, it's just faster or you can't waste any space in your bag. But it's not all the time and not true for everyone."

"I like you naked," he said, expression now a goofy smile.

"I like you naked too, but right now I need you dressed, so lift your arms." He did, and I pulled his t-shirt down over his torso.

"All right." I tugged on his hand. "It's time for us to go."

"Where?"

"Just next door."

"I don't have to talk to anyone, do I?"

"No, I wouldn't do that to you." As I led him down the hall, I explained, "I'm watching my neighbor's condo while she's away. She needed someone to water plants and feed her fish. She also happens to have an amazing Jacuzzi."

His eyes widened. "Really?"

"Yes."

"And you're allowed to use it?"

I nodded.

"With me?"

"She didn't tell me not to bring anyone over, and I thought you were too tired for more sex anyway."

He smiled. "I might get inspired."

I unlocked the door and grabbed his hand. "Come in."

The condo was a mirror image of mine. I led Sean to the bathroom and turned on the water to let it heat up. When I was satisfied with the temperature, I closed the drain and turned to Sean. "Strip."

"That sounds a lot like the start of our evening."

I grinned as I pushed my sweats over my hips. "It does, doesn't it?"

The tub filled quickly, and I gestured for Sean to go ahead and step in. He groaned as he sank down into the warm water. "That feels so good."

The husky tone of his voice made my cock stir, despite the explosive sex we'd just had. I looked up, and I saw him watching me.

"You're so fucking sexy."

I gave a dismissive wave. For some reason the compliment had embarrassment heating my face.

Sean frowned. "Seriously? Have you seen yourself?"

"I work out from habit, because not being in shape risked my life and the lives of the men on my team."

"You really don't get it, do you?"

Apparently, I didn't, because I had no idea what he was talking about.

"It's not just your body. I mean, yeah, it's hot as fuck, but you have this presence, this way of making people want to please you, not because they're scared, but because you believe in them. You must have been an amazing motivator for the younger members of your team."

"I'm good at making people do what I say. That's part of why—"

"No. You're good at making people *want* to do what you say, but you only use that power for good. That's why I trust you, and why it doesn't freak me out to call you Daddy. I know you'll take care of me. I trust you to know what I need. I've never had that from anyone before."

"Wow. I... Thank you." I had no idea he saw me that way. I had leadership skills and strength. I could make people follow me, but I'd never had a lover say anything like that. My heart was pounding harder than if I'd just run ten miles uphill.

"Are you going to get in the tub with me?" Sean asked. "Because I kind of thought that was the point."

"Brat." I slapped my hand across the water, splashing him, even though I was thankful for the change of subject. "You're going to be in trouble for that."

"Good trouble?" His impish smile made me want to start some trouble right then.

"If me making you wait so long you're crying for the right to come is good trouble, then yes."

He gasped in obviously pretend shock. "You wouldn't."

"I think you know I would," I said as I stepped into the tub. "Are you ready for me to turn the jets on?"

"Oh, I forgot that part. See how distracting you are?"

I lay back against the side of the tub, and he shifted position until he was between my legs. "I guess you can do anything you want."

I shook my head. "I can't stop thinking about you."

I watched the muscles of his throat work as he swallowed. "That's… wow."

"I know I promised you I wouldn't push, but—"

"You know I made you promise that because I can't stop thinking about you, and that scares the hell out of me."

I pulled him to me and kissed the curve of his shoulder. "Thank you for trusting me enough to tell me that."

I turned him around in my arms so his back was against my chest, and he let his head rest on my shoulder. We were silent for several moments, then he said, "My dad was older and way richer than my mom. After they got married, he showered her with gifts and took her around the world. They lived in a huge house with servants, and she loved it. But after I was born, he decided she wasn't as beautiful anymore, and he didn't like how much time she spent with me. He wanted to hire a nanny so she could travel with him, but she wanted me to come along. She wanted to truly be a family."

Sean took a deep breath, and I held him tightly against me. I could guess where this was going.

"He kicked her out and made sure she got nothing. She'd signed a prenup, thinking it was silly because they'd always be together."

I kissed the top of his head. "I'm so sorry."

"Thanks. My mom hasn't dated anyone seriously since. She won't risk being hurt again. She changed herself a lot for my dad, pretended to like things she didn't, shit like that. Basically, she did whatever he wanted. So she taught me to guard my heart and always be me. She told me I had to do what I want and never to just accept something. But now I realize it's made me restless and indecisive, because I'm always questioning whether what I have is what I really want."

"So that's why you haven't settled into a career or…"

"Gotten my fucking act together?"

I hugged him tighter. "No, I was going to say, had a relationship."

"I guess I'm pretty fucked up."

"No more than most people, and recognizing what you've been doing is huge."

He sighed as he played with my hands, tracing my palm and each finger. "I haven't done anything to change it."

"You're here right now, aren't you? You didn't run away when I mentioned feelings."

"I guess."

I ran my hands over his chest, dragging my fingers across his nipples and making him groan. "Yes, definitely here."

"Just because I'm not running doesn't mean I'm okay."

I let my hands glide up and down his wet torso, trying to soothe him. "I think you're amazing and brave, and I only ever want you to change things about yourself that you want to change."

"I know. You said you wanted the real me. You're just forcing me to admit who I really am." He turned around and straddled my lap. I could see concern in his eyes, but also heat.

"I know you said we were here to relax, but I need to kiss you."

"Then kiss me."

Our lips met, and it was the warmest, most comforting kiss I'd ever experienced.

When Sean pulled away, he looked like he wanted to say something. I kissed along his jaw, and then whispered in his ear, "Whatever you're thinking, just take a deep breath and tell me when you're ready."

He nodded and shifted so we were looking at each other. "Blake, I…"

"Yes?"

"I thought I shouldn't want what I have with you, but why shouldn't I if it's right for me, for us."

I needed a steadying breath before I spoke. "I want this too."

He turned around again and settled against me. I held him as the warm water swirled around us. When our skin started to prune, I helped him out of the tub. We didn't say much as we dressed and returned to my condo.

Sean was loose-limbed, and he seemed ready to fall asleep. "Do you want to stay?"

"Yes, but can we get in bed now while we're all soft and warm?"

"Do you want me to just hold you or do you want more? We can do whatever you choose."

"Right now, I'm not sure."

"Okay, brush your teeth, get ready for bed, and then we'll see."

Sean was already in bed by the time I'd finished in the bathroom. I lifted the covers and slid in beside him. When I spooned against him, he wriggled until he'd fit my cock into the seam of his ass.

I growled and pumped my hips, rubbing against him. "Is this what you want?"

"Yes, but after what I said earlier, this all feels scary right now."

"What if we do this without any role play, no expectations that you submit to me, just me and you, and what we each need."

He turned over to face me. "Yes, please. That."

I kissed him, and he kissed me back, biting at my lower lip like he wanted to consume me. He grabbed my ass, pulling me to him until our cocks were sliding against one another as he frantically worked his hips. But I needed more friction, so I rolled onto my back and pulled him on top of me. He rutted against me hard as I held his hips, thrusting up. We were both gasping for breath when he finally sat back.

I tugged on his ass, encouraging him to move. "I want to suck your cock."

"Oh, fuck." He straddled my shoulders and braced himself on the headboard as I stroked him. Then he angled himself so he could rub the tip of his cock over my lips.

"More," I gasped. He lowered himself, and I teased his slit and sucked on his head. "You can fuck my mouth. It's okay."

"Are you sure?"

"Yes, please. Just let go."

He pushed into me, still using careful strokes but going deeper now. I savored the taste of him and used my tongue to drive him insane. I could tell he was close when he pulled out and stared down at me, wide-eyed. "I want you inside me when I come."

"Yes. I want that too." I reached out blindly, trying to get to the nightstand drawer. Something crashed to the floor, but I didn't care. I got the drawer open and grabbed what we needed.

Sean took the lube from me and coated his fingers. Then he rose up on his knees, and my brain short-circuited as I watched him push those digits inside himself. I was definitely going to have him do this for me again. He was so fucking hot, stretching himself with his head dropped back. He drove his fingers in as deep as they could go.

"So good. Keep fucking yourself like that."

"You like watching?"

"Fuck, yes."

He indulged me for a few more seconds, then he pulled his fingers from his body and grabbed the condom. I watched as he rolled the latex over my dick. When he added more lube and stroked me, I arched up, driving my cock into his hand. "Need you."

"Now who's eager?"

I huffed. "I'm always eager for you."

He looked down at me, his expression more serious than I would've expected. "Really?"

"Yes. How can you not know that?"

"But you make me wait, and you don't even seem affected. It's so easy for you."

"Easy? Sometimes I'm afraid I'll come before I ever get inside. I'm just good at pretending I'm not about to blow."

"Don't do that now. Let me see how much you want me."

I growled. "Ride me, Sean. Right fucking now."

He laughed as he took my cock and guided it to his hole.

When he sank down enough for me to push into him, I groaned. "More."

"Maybe I want to tease you. I don't get that chance often."

"You could do it more often if you wanted to."

He shook his head. "I love what you do to me. This is just something I want occasionally, having you under me like this, at my mercy."

"Fuck me, Sean. Right fucking now."

"You need this?" He lowered himself a little more.

I gritted my teeth. "Sean."

He rose almost all the way off and then lowered himself again, taking me an inch at a time.

"You better not stop."

"I don't have to take your orders right now."

I drove up into him as I held him tight. "No, but you have to take my cock."

"Arrogant bastard."

"You fucking love it."

A sound of pure joy escaped him. "Yeah, I do."

He leaned forward, bracing himself on my shoulders and working his hips in a circular motion. I could feel his precum as he rubbed his cock on my stomach.

"So good," I groaned.

"Always good with you."

He started fucking himself on me in earnest then, and I drove my hips up, pushing as deep as I could go.

"More, Blake. Give me more."

I sat up and gripped his ass, so I could lift him and bring him back down. He arched his back and clung to my neck. "God, yes, right there. Yes!"

"Come for me, baby. Come all over me. I need to see you."

"Want to drive you crazy, Blake."

"You are. I'm so close, but I need you to come first. Need to take care of you."

"So good. Such a good Daddy."

I loved that he'd forgotten we weren't role playing, that calling me Daddy came naturally to him now. I wrapped my hand around his cock and jerked him off.

"Fuck, Blake, fuck. I need…" He cried out, and his cum shot between us, coating my hand and spattering my torso.

When he'd wrung himself dry, I rolled us so he was lying on his back. Then I pulled out and stripped off the condom. "I want to cover you with my cum, boy."

"Please, Daddy. Please come on me."

I pumped my cock. Faster. Faster. My balls tightened and heat shot through me. "Mine," I shouted as the first jet of cum landed on his chest.

"Thank you, Daddy. I love you, Daddy."

My body jerked, shooting again and again. Had he really said that?

When I'd finished, I looked at him, and the horror in his eyes told me I hadn't misheard. "Don't panic."

"I don't… I didn't…"

"It's okay. We don't have to talk about it now."

Sean looked down at his chest, which was covered with both our seed.

I bent and ran my tongue through it, hoping that would distract him. "Kiss me," he ordered.

I did, letting him taste us both as I stretched out over him, anchoring him with my weight. I wanted to tell him I loved him too. And that I'd been hoping he was falling for me, because I never wanted this thing between us to end. But I knew he wasn't ready to hear those things. I wasn't sure when he would be. I rolled to my back and pulled him with me. He nestled against me as I petted him, stroking his hair and his back. Eventually, he drifted to sleep.

He stirred about an hour later, and I knew the moment he remembered what had happened before he'd fallen asleep.

His body went rigid. He sat up and swung his legs over the side of the bed, without looking at me. So much for hoping he'd spend the night with me.

"I need to go. I have to think, and I can't do that here."

"Okay." I could feel tension radiating from him. I sat up, running my hand through my hair. "I'll drive you home."

"No, my car's here. I'll drive myself."

"But you're upset, and I—"

"I'm fine."

"Sean, you're not fine."

He sighed. "Okay. I'm not, but I'm also not as upset as you probably think I am."

"You're not?"

"No. I meant what I said earlier, but this is all happening so fast, and I just need some time alone."

"I understand, but you asked me to take care of you, and I don't want you driving when you're worried like this."

He turned to look at me, and I saw tears in his eyes. "You're so good to me. I know that, but there's still a part of me that wants to fight it."

I nodded. "It's okay that you feel like that?"

"Yeah? Because I want to be good, I really do."

I moved closer to him, so I could reach up and cup his face. "You are. You're my good boy, even if you need space and you're stubborn and want to drive yourself."

He smiled, and I thought he relaxed a bit.

I debated how far I should go and finally decided he needed to know how I felt before he left. "I love you too. You don't have to respond, but I want you to know."

He nodded. "I… Wow, I didn't mean for this to happen."

"I know you didn't. But love isn't something you can control. It's not like learning to hold back an orgasm. We don't have that kind of control over falling for someone."

"Some of us regular humans don't have that kind of control over orgasms either."

I laughed. "You're getting better at it, boy."

"Thank you."

I missed the "Daddy" he might have added earlier in the evening.

He stood and started getting dressed. "I'll call you soon. I promise."

I nodded. I wanted to give him a deadline or tell him I'd call him instead. But I had to let him do this on his own. He needed to think and be sure about what he could handle. I just had to hope he loved me too much not to come back to me.

16

SEAN

Avery scowled at me. "You're driving me crazy."

"What am I doing?"

"You're way too jittery. You haven't stopped moving all morning."

"Of course I'm moving. We're packing. That requires me to walk around."

"You know what I mean."

I did. I'd been unsettled for the last week and a half. I'd called Blake to let him know I'd gotten home safely after I'd spilled my secrets to him, and we'd had a few brief text exchanges. Otherwise I hadn't spoken to him since I asked for time to think. I missed him, but I was scared about seeing him at Avery and Graham's housewarming party. God only knew what else would spill from my mouth.

I realized I was bouncing on my toes as I taped up a box. Avery was right. I couldn't be still, but I had good reason to be a nervous wreck. Avery was moving out, and I was going to be alone. I'd told Blake I loved him, and I was about to see him again for the first time since then.

"I just wish things were like they used to be."

Avery frowned. "You mean like when we used to go out, get fucked by random guys, and then spend the next weekend complaining about men and binge-watching *Charmed*?"

"Um… Yes?"

"No, you don't."

I gave a dramatic sigh. By the time I'd filled another box, I couldn't take it anymore, so I blurted out my real problem. "I accidentally told Blake I love him."

Avery dropped the roll of packing tape he was holding. "You did what?"

"You know that haze after you've come so hard you think you're literally going to die?"

Avery smiled. "Yeah."

"I was floating there, and Blake came all over me, and it felt so good and—"

Avery held up his hands. "TMI."

"I've seen you get spanked, so don't even start with me."

Avery rolled his eyes.

"Everything was perfect, and the words just slipped out."

"What did he say?"

"Don't panic."

Avery pressed his lips together, obviously trying not to laugh.

"Go ahead and make fun. I know how ridiculous that is."

"It's just that he knows you so well."

Avery was right about that. "He didn't push me to say anything else. He just held me."

"And then?" Avery made a rolling motion with his hand, obviously impatient for me to go on.

"I fell asleep, and when I woke up, I panicked."

"Did you run out on him?"

I shook my head. "I told him I needed some time to think. I even called him when I got back here."

"So that's why you did that," Avery said. "I wondered what was up."

"He didn't think I should drive because I was upset."

Avery studied me for a moment as if expecting me to say more. "You didn't tell him to fuck off?"

"No. I thought it was sweet."

Avery pretended he was about to faint. "I never thought I'd see the day. You really are in love with him."

I flipped him off. "Blake told me he loved me too. He said he couldn't let me leave without saying it."

"And you haven't seen him since then?" Avery looked like he might be about to start on a rant.

"I really did need to think."

"No wonder you're all jittery."

I was sure I'd been hell to live with that week. "I'm sorry I'm such a fucking mess. You're moving in with Graham, and that's a huge deal for you. I should be a better friend."

Avery left the box he was working on and walked over to me. "This move is a big deal for you too. It would be even if you weren't worried about things with Blake. You could have told me not to invite him today, you know."

"No, I couldn't. Everyone would ask questions, and the thing is, I want him there. I'm just scared."

He studied me for a moment as if trying to decide what to say. "Have you renewed the lease yet?"

I shook my head.

"You know it's due in four days, right?"

"Of course I do."

"Sean—"

"I'll make a decision by then, okay?"

"Okay. Let's get these in the car. We need to get going." I could tell it was killing him not to push me harder.

I picked up a box and followed him to the parking lot. Even with most of his stuff already at the new house or sitting in his trunk, I still couldn't believe he wouldn't be living with me anymore.

"Avery?"

"Yeah?"

"Thank you for being the best roommate ever."

I hugged him and pretended I wasn't crying—over his leaving, over Blake, over the mess of my life that I really wanted to fix.

17

BLAKE

"YOU'RE UNUSUALLY QUIET TODAY. Are you all right?" Leo and I had been going over some security plans for Thrust, but now it was time to head to Avery and Graham's housewarming party. Leo was never a particularly talkative man, but he hadn't said a word that wasn't related to business all afternoon.

"I'm fine. Just thinking through the suggestions you gave me."

I could tell he was lying, but I also knew there was no point in pushing him. If he didn't want to talk, he wouldn't.

"What about you?" he asked as we got into his truck. "How are things with Sean?"

I frowned. I had my own reasons to be tense today. I hadn't seen Sean in over a week, and there was the potential for things to be awkward between us at the party. "Unsettled."

Leo snorted. "That boy needs to realize you're perfect for him. If I were you, I'd put him over my knee and spank him until he confessed how much he needs you. Then I'd edge him until he promised never to walk way."

I couldn't help but smile at Leo's suggestions. "I've managed the first part already, but with the second, force isn't going to work with Sean."

Leo sighed. "I know. I was joking, mostly. But if he's at least admitted to wanting you for more than your cock, things aren't too bad."

"They weren't, but then he said more than he meant to, and he asked for some time to think about where things are going for us."

Leo frowned. "From what Avery tells me, as soon as something starts to seem difficult or serious, Sean backs away, whether it's work or school or a man."

"That's how he's reacted in the past."

Leo glanced at the GPS and took the next turn. "You're determined to be an exception?"

"I am."

"You really have fallen for him then, huh?"

I drew in a deep breath as I took in the view of the mountains in the distance. "I have, but he's skittish and I've been literally treating him like a jumpy pony."

Leo chuckled. "Any chance you'd like to show off your work at our fall demo night? I don't have anyone lined up for pony play."

I thought about Sean's reaction when I mentioned him wearing the tail plug at Thrust. "Possibly. I'll talk to Sean about it."

"Good. Don't give up on him."

No way in hell would I do that.

"He needs you, and I can tell he makes you happy. You've smiled a hell of a lot more since you started seeing him."

But Leo had been smiling a lot less lately. "What's the real reason you were being quiet earlier?"

He sighed. "It's no big deal. There's a sub I really like, he wanted me to train him, but things got too intense too fast, and he's… It just wasn't right."

I had a feeling there was a lot more to the story than Leo was saying. "Not right like you weren't a good fit or…"

"It was inappropriate. I should never have agreed to take him on."

"Is he an employee or something?"

Leo tapped his fingers on the steering wheel as he waited for the light to turn. "Something like that. It's…"

"Complicated?"

Leo laughed. "You could say that. And he's young, really young."

"That hasn't mattered for me or Graham."

"He's younger than Sean and Avery."

I glanced over and saw that Leo was blushing. That was something I hadn't seen before. "Still, that doesn't mean it won't work. You said it was intense, but was it good?"

He sighed. "It was exquisite. I haven't experienced anything like it in years."

"So?"

"It was a mistake, and I can't see him again, not like that. He needs someone younger, someone who… isn't me."

"Or maybe you're exactly what he needs, and he's what you've been looking for." I wasn't sure why I felt the need to push, but I did. Something told me Leo needed to pursue this.

He snorted. "I never expected a SEAL to be such a romantic sap."

"Sorry to ruin the stereotype for you."

"We're almost there. They live on the next street."

I decided to let him get away with the change of subject. "I can't wait to see their house. I've heard a lot about it from Sean."

"It's gorgeous, and there will be tons of food. Avery's

friend Felicity and her mom are bringing lots of sides, and Graham's ordered a cake from Avery's favorite bakery."

That all sounded fantastic, but Leo's expression didn't match his words. Something told me he wasn't looking forward to this party. Maybe he was worried he'd see less of his best friend now that Graham would be living with Avery, or he was just feeling down about the guy he thought was wrong for him. I couldn't think of any other reason for him to dread hanging out with Graham.

SEAN

When Avery and I arrived, Blake was already there. He turned when I shut the car door, and his face lit up with a smile. Nervous warmth spread through me, and I smiled back.

"That right there," Avery said. "That's the look I meant. Don't fuck things up."

"Hush," I hissed, not wanting someone else to overhear.

Avery just laughed as he opened the trunk. Graham came down the steps to greet us, and Blake followed.

"You need some help?" Blake asked as Graham pulled Avery in for a kiss.

"Sure. Thanks." My hands were sweaty, and I almost dropped the box I'd pulled from the trunk as I tried to hand it to Blake. Why was I so nervous?

Because you really want to move in with him.

"Are you okay?" Blake asked.

"Yeah. It's… um… it's good to see you."

"It's good to see you too."

A moan from Avery interrupted us, and Blake laughed.

"Get a room," I shouted.

"Seriously," Leo said as he came to join us. He grabbed one of the boxes Avery and Graham had been ignoring.

Graham waved a hand dismissively. "You've seen plenty of that at Thrust."

"This isn't a club," Leo snapped before stomping away with the box.

"Whoa," Avery said. "What's up with him?"

"He's been in a bad mood for the last few weeks," Graham said. "I've tried to talk to him, but he won't tell me what's wrong."

Blake looked like he was about to say something, but he glanced toward Leo's retreating form and stayed silent.

"You know something," I said.

He frowned. "Maybe."

"Spill it."

"I'm not sure he'd want me to."

"I'm worried about him," Graham said. "Just tell me if he's okay."

Blake sighed. "There's a guy he thinks is too young and somehow wrong for him. But he likes the guy a lot."

"How young is he?" I asked, knowing Leo didn't care about Graham and Avery's twenty-year age gap.

"I'm not sure. All he said was that he's younger than you."

Graham frowned. "I'll try to talk to him again later. Maybe with enough whiskey in him he'll open up. I've stocked up on the good stuff."

Avery rolled his eyes. "If you two get started it will be a very long night."

"There's a room waiting for you at my place," I said. Having to say my, not ours, hurt even more than I expected.

"You still haven't found a roommate?" Blake asked.

"No. I'm… uh… working on it."

Avery made a sound between a scoff and a laugh.

"Behave, boy," Graham said, looking at him sternly.

"Yes, Daddy."

"Let's get these inside before my arms give out." I didn't want to see any more of Avery and Graham's cuteness right then.

Once we'd set the boxes down in the living room, Blake and I went to the kitchen for a drink. Graham's daughter Mandy was there, mixing up a pitcher of something I hoped was highly alcoholic.

I laid a hand on Blake's arm. "Have you met Mandy?"

"I just did right before you got here."

"Would you like a drink?" Mandy asked. "This is black-berry whiskey lemonade."

I nodded. "Fuck, yes."

"That sounds amazing," Blake said.

"Are Wren and Carter here yet?" I asked while Mandy poured the drinks.

"Wren is. He's been tasked with assembling a shelf upstairs, and Carter should be here any time. He was picking up Felicity and her mom and grandma." She turned to Blake then. "Were you working the concert at Biltmore yesterday?"

He nodded. "My firm just signed a contract with them. I don't usually handle concerts myself, but they requested my presence specifically, and they're not a client I'd say no to."

"I guess not," I said. Biltmore was the largest employer in town.

Felicity, Carter, Felicity's mom, Dawn, and Felicity's grandma arrived a few minutes later. Wren came down and Mandy brought the drink pitcher onto the porch. Chaos ensued as introductions were made, and all the food they'd brought was taken in and arranged on the kitchen counter. Dawn had brought one of her famous lemon cakes, and I was thrilled that I'd be able to introduce Blake to their amaz-ingness.

Felicity started directing everyone to get more space

cleared in the living room and start working on preparations for dinner. While she divvied up the tasks and made sure everyone had seen the house, I noticed Wren watching Leo rather intently. Not that I blamed him; Leo was hot as hell. If Avery hadn't told me Leo didn't put up with brattiness and had a thing for pain sluts, I would've offered to spread my ass for him seconds after we met.

But Wren's expression was more worried than lustful. Then Leo looked up and noticed Wren staring, and Wren turned around so quickly he turned over a side table.

"Sorry. I... Sorry."

He hurried from the room, and that's when it clicked. Blake had said Leo was hung up over a man who was too young and not right for him. *Holy shit.*

I glanced at Avery and Graham, but fortunately, neither of them seemed to have noticed what I had. The only other person who was watching Wren was Mandy. I wondered if she'd guessed as well.

A few moments later, Blake headed out to the deck to help set up all the chairs people had brought, and I ended up in the kitchen helping Felicity put chips and dip into bowls while Avery showed Felicity's mother and grandmother the rest of the house.

"Tell me you're going to hold onto Blake by any means necessary," Felicity said as she handed me a bag of tortilla chips.

I narrowed my eyes. "What has Avery told you?"

"Not as much as I wanted to know. And he totally undersold Blake, by the way. That man is fucking swoon worthy."

I grinned. "Damn right he is."

She studied me for a moment as I dumped a jar of salsa into a small bowl. "Have you got a roommate yet?"

"No."

"Mmm-hmm."

I hated that knowing tone.

"When is the lease due to be renewed?"

Why did I feel like she already knew and was just testing me? "Four days, but I'll have it figured out, okay?"

"So you haven't asked Blake about moving in with him?"

"Avery clearly has told you too much."

She narrowed her eyes. "Have you seen how Blake looks at you?"

"I get it. You and Avery think I need to talk to him, but—" The chip bag I'd been struggling with suddenly exploded, and chips went everywhere. "Shit!"

I scrambled to pick them up, but Felicity stopped me with a hand on my arm.

"Go find him."

"Now?" My voice came out as a squeak.

"I know you. You'll put it off until the last second, and if you do you'll be stuck signing the lease when you really don't want to."

I hated how right she was. "You think you know everything, don't you?"

She just smirked at me. "It's my best quality."

"Bitch."

"Asshole," Felicity said. "I'll take care of the chips. Go find your man and talk to him."

"I need a minute first."

"Sean."

"Please let me do this my way." Felicity and Avery meant well, but the thought of talking to Blake right then made my stomach churn.

"All right, but you better not leave this party without telling Blake what you want."

"Did Avery put you up to this?"

"He didn't have to. You do know I worry about you too, right?"

As much as Felicity and I gave each other shit, I knew she did. But I wasn't going to let her think I liked it. "The two of you suck."

"Get." She shooed me out of the kitchen.

Since I was fairly certain Blake was out back and I wasn't prepared to see him with Felicity's words echoing in my head, I headed for the front porch. I found Wren there, sitting in the swing, a fluffy tortoiseshell cat I didn't recognize on his lap.

"Did they get a cat?" Avery hadn't mentioned it, and Graham totally struck me as a dog person.

"No, it wandered up, but it's really sweet." He scratched the animal's ears, and it purred.

I sat on the railing near the swing. "Is this crowd too much for you?"

"Nah, I'm just having a weird day."

"Because of your dad and Avery?"

He shook his head. "No. That's all fine. I mean the whole thing was a little weird at first, but Avery's great."

I nodded. "He is."

"Are you sad about him moving out?"

"Yeah."

"But you have Blake now so you won't be lonely."

"True." He was right. I did have Blake. At least until I fucked it up.

Wren stroked the cat's back, and it arched into his hand. "That must be nice."

"Having a boyfriend?"

"Having a man who looks at you like Blake does, one who'll admit that he wants to be with you."

Oh, shit. I was fairly sure I knew where this was going, but I had to pretend I didn't. I gave Wren an appreciative once-over, not being the least bit subtle. It was no hardship, since he was as hot as his father. "I wouldn't think you'd have any trouble finding a man who was interested."

He scowled. "Interested in fucking, sure, but—Shit. Just ignore me. You don't want to hear all this. You should head out back, it's a lot more fun around there."

As if to punctuate his statement, laughter echoed around the side of the house. I could smell the burgers cooking, and it made my stomach rumble, but despite that, I wanted to stay right where I was.

"I'm not feeling too celebratory. I'm happy for Avery and Graham, but I'm feeling kind of mixed up right now."

Wren sighed. "Yeah, me too."

"School shit?"

"No, school's great, actually. I... God, it sounds so stupid." The cat stirred and started kneading his lap.

"What does?"

Wren shook his head. "You really don't have to listen to this."

"If I go out there," I tilted my head toward the back of the house, "I'm going to have to face some of my own shit. Trust me, I'm happy to listen."

Wren smiled. "If facing your own shit means asking Blake if you can move in with him, then you better do it."

"Jesus, even you know."

He laughed. "Felicity's my sister-in-law. There's not much I don't know."

"Fine, you already know my secret, so tell me yours."

"I decided to start this architecture program at the last minute because there's a man I like who lives in Charlotte."

Oh, fuck. I was right. This was going to rock Graham's world when it came out.

"And?"

"It's a good thing I'm loving school, because the thing with the guy is going nowhere."

"Yeah? That sucks."

Wren sighed. "He's older, and he thinks I'm not right for him, and I get why, but I just don't care. I want him anyway."

My heart pounded. Should I tell him I knew? I glanced toward the screen door and then out into the yard. I didn't see anyone nearby.

"Wren, I think I know who the man is."

His eyes grew huge. "What? How?"

"When you fell over the table earlier, I saw who you were looking at."

"Oh, fuck!" The cat jumped from his lap and ran.

Wren looked like he might follow it, but I sat down beside him and put a hand on his arm. "I don't think anyone else noticed, except maybe Mandy. Graham and Avery were too caught up in each other and their excitement about the house."

Wren shook his head. "I should go. I didn't want to come, knowing he'd be here, but I didn't know how to say no when it was so important to my dad."

I knew I was probably overstepping my bounds, but Avery had warned me about Leo, so I thought I should warn Wren too. "You do know about the kinky stuff Leo likes, right?"

He made a disgusted sound. "I might be the baby of the family, but I'm not as naive as some people think I am."

"I don't think you're naive or too young or anything else. I just wanted to check."

He sighed. "You probably still think he was right to reject me."

"I'm not sure there's a clear right or wrong for the two of you, but I get why he's skittish."

Wren huffed. "I don't know that I'd use that word for him."

"No?"

"He's so fucking sure of himself."

Did he really not know how much he'd affected Leo? "From what Blake and Graham have said, Leo's not been himself for weeks. He's fucked up over this too."

Wren looked so damn hopeful then, and I wondered if I'd done the right thing by telling him. "I get why he said we can't keep seeing each other, but I can't stop wanting him."

"*Keep* seeing each other?"

"We… um… saw each other a few times." He said "saw" in a way that made it obvious it was a euphemism for fucking.

I smiled. "Is he as hot as I think he would be?"

"Hotter."

"Holy fuck."

"Sean? Are you in here?" It was Blake.

"I'm on the porch." I glanced at Wren and whispered, "I won't say anything."

"Thank you," he mouthed back.

Blake pushed the screen door open and stepped onto the porch. "What are you two doing out here? We're ready to eat."

"Wren was making friends with a neighborhood cat, and we were just talking."

Blake glanced around like he was searching for Wren's new friend.

"The cat ran off a few minutes ago," Wren said.

"Oh. Well, do you want to come eat?"

"Sure." I stood and headed for the door.

I heard the swing creak as Wren got to his feet. "I… um… I need to go. Can you tell my dad something came up? A project for school."

"Sure," I said.

"Thanks."

He started down the steps, but I called out, "Wait. Give me your number."

He did, and I added him to my contacts, then sent him a text. "Call me. I'm a decent listener."

"Okay."

If he didn't call me soon, I'd call him instead.

"Is he all right?" Blake asked when we stepped inside.

"Yeah, mostly." I'd told Wren I wouldn't say anything, but I was bursting to tell someone, and I absolutely couldn't tell Avery. "You know how you said Leo was into a younger guy, but the guy wasn't right for him for some reason?"

"Yes." Blake looked at me, then his eyes widened. "No way."

I nodded.

"Oh, fuck."

"Yeah, that's about right."

After we'd eaten, Graham and Carter played Leo and Blake in a fierce game of sweaty, shirtless volleyball. I would've been happy to watch them all day. When they finally ended the match with Blake and Leo winning the final game of five, I noticed Avery and Felicity huddled together. Avery looked away quickly when he saw me staring. They were definitely conspiring. No way in hell was I going to let them decide my future.

I walked up to Blake and Graham. Both of them were still shirtless, and my cock was more than a little interested by the time I reached Blake's side and took hold of his arm. "Can I borrow him?"

Graham chuckled. "Be my guest."

"I saw you watching me," Blake said as we walked away.

"Damn right I was watching. If I could've gotten away with it, I would've jerked off while I did."

"Sean!"

"I'm kidding. Sort of."

Blake raised his brows. "So what are you borrowing me for?"

"Did you see the upstairs?" I was stalling, but I would ask him eventually.

"I got a tour when I first arrived, since you and Avery were late."

He emphasized the last word, and I could swear my ass stung just from the thought of him spanking me. "That wasn't my fault."

He didn't look at all convinced.

"Okay, maybe it was a little, but Avery and I were talking and getting all mushy. I'm going to miss him."

Blake pulled me into his arms, giving me a tight hug. "You're forgiven."

"Are you sure you saw all the rooms upstairs?"

"What is going on?"

Fuck it. I had to just do this. "I want to talk to you, and I don't want anyone to bother us while I do."

"Then let's go."

I led him up the stairs and into one of the guest bedrooms where I shut the door behind us and locked it.

Blake raised his brow. "I thought you wanted to talk."

There was a really nice bed in here, and it was already made up. Seducing him would be so much easier than talking.

"Don't even think about it, boy."

"Make me."

He looked confused. "Make you what?"

"Make me tell you, make me talk to you. I need to know you won't let me get out of it."

"Baby." He stepped closer and cupped my face. "Are you okay?"

"I will be if I can manage to say this."

Blake sat on the bed and pulled me down onto his lap.

He took my chin in his hand and turned me so I was looking at him. His eyes held me in that intense way he had, but it wasn't unnerving anymore, it was comforting.

"Talk."

"Um… I…"

"You clearly have something important to tell me, boy. Tell me now, or I'll have to punish you later when I'd rather enjoy you."

"Yes, Daddy." I could breathe again after saying those words. "I don't have a roommate, and I have to sign a new lease in four days."

He raised his brow. "Why didn't you tell me that before now?"

"I told you I hadn't found a roommate."

"But not about the lease. Didn't you think that was something I should know? Preventing his boy from putting off things like this is what a Daddy is for."

I looked down and nodded. "I know."

"So why did you wait to talk to me?"

"Because I knew what I wanted, but I didn't want to ask for it."

"And what is it that you want?"

I couldn't read Blake's expression, but I plunged ahead anyway. "I want to move in with you."

BLAKE

I LET out the breath I'd been holding. He'd said exactly what I'd hoped he would. "You do?"

"Yes. I want to sleep in your bed every night and have you there to remind me to be good, to spank me, to keep me in line. I want to surrender to you. I want you to be my Daddy."

I hadn't been sure I would ever hear Sean state what he needed so plainly. "Thank you for telling me that. I need to take care of you, to watch you become more disciplined, to fuck you until you can't breathe" —I loved how those words made his eyes go wide— "and to love you."

"Oh, wow." He looked stunned. I held onto him, concerned his legs would give out.

"I hope that wasn't too much, because there's no going back for me. I started falling for you the first night we were together."

"Me too." His voice was shaky, but he kept going. "That's why I fought you so hard, and why I still fight sometimes. But even when I'm resisting you, I still love you."

My heart skipped a beat. "Sean, you don't have to—"

"This time I meant to say it. I do love you, and it's stupid to pretend I don't. I want to move in with you because I love you. Well, that and the hot sex."

"We wouldn't want to discount that."

He frowned at me, looking worried. "So…?"

"So what?"

"Can I move in? I mean, it's okay if you don't think we're ready. I can try to negotiate a shorter lease."

I kissed him, soft and sweet and then harder, nipping at his bottom lip before pulling back.

"Of course you can move in. I thought my answer was obvious. I would've asked you to before now, but I thought you needed to come to that decision on your own."

"I didn't really, though. Avery and Felicity pushed me to talk to you."

"Had you thought about it before they mentioned it?"

He nodded.

"Then they just gave you encouragement."

"I was afraid they were going to ask you for me if I didn't hurry up."

I laughed. "Leo told me I should edge you until you agreed to move in."

"What?"

"He was joking. He just wants us to be happy."

"From what Graham says, he always wants what's good for other people, but I think he needs to spend some time making himself happy."

"So you think he should be with Wren?"

He frowned. "Maybe. Do you think it's wrong?"

"Wrong, no. Complicated, yes. But I kind of have the feeling it's inevitable."

"Like us?"

His words warmed me all the way to my toes. I pulled him to me for another kiss, but someone pounded on the door.

"You better not be fucking in there," Avery yelled. "We get to try out every room first."

"So what if we are?" Sean said. "You're the one who told me I had to talk to Blake."

"Did you?"

"Yes."

"And?"

"I won't be renewing the lease."

"Did you hear that?" Avery called.

I heard a muffled squeak. Then Graham said, "Sorry for the interruption. Carry on."

Footsteps receded, followed by loud laughter downstairs.

Sean looked at me, and I could tell he was thinking about doing exactly what Graham suggested.

"No. We're going to congratulate Graham and Avery on the house and offer to help them unpack tomorrow. Then we're going to your apartment where you will pack enough things for the next few days. After that, I'm taking you home."

"Home?"

I nodded. "Yes."

"Okay."

I studied him for a moment. "That's it? No protest?"

"None. See what a good boy I am?"

That feigned innocence wouldn't get him anywhere with me. "What exactly do you think will happen when I get you to our condo?"

"Something amazing."

I would make him feel amazing, but I hadn't forgotten that he'd waited to tell me about the lease and about what he really wanted.

W hen we got back to my apartment, Sean was quiet as we stepped inside, seeming to anticipate what I wanted from him. "Are you ready to surrender to me, boy?"

"Yes, sir."

I look hold of both his hands. "I love that you can finally admit what you want."

"What I want is you, Daddy."

"I want you too. But first we need to talk about how you resisted asking to move in."

Sean looked down at his feet. "Are you going to punish me, Daddy?"

"Do you want me to?"

"I think I need you to."

I remembered how, when we'd first gotten together, he'd insisted that his desire to be spanked was nothing more than a game. "You've come such a long way, boy."

"Thank you, Daddy."

I cupped his cheek and kissed him softly. I had to force myself to pull back before I was really ready. But I had plans for us, and there would be plenty of time for sweet kisses later.

"Go into our bedroom, strip, and lay over the end of the bed."

"Yes, sir." His tone held no hint of mockery like it used to, but there was a wicked smile on his face. He knew he was going to love this as much as I would. That thought sent warmth rushing through me. I had wanted a relationship like this for so long. And once I met Sean, I wanted it with him. At first, I didn't think that would be possible, but now I was glad I'd stayed hopeful. I was a very lucky man, and once I punished Sean thoroughly, I'd make sure he was just as happy as I was.

I gathered the supplies I needed and joined him in the

bedroom. My first glimpse of him had me sucking in my breath. His arms were stretched toward the top of the bed, and his back was deeply arched so his ass tilted up. He knew how much I liked him to display it for me.

"You look so hot like that, boy. I'm going to fuck you until you scream, but first I'm going to make you come."

"You're not going to spank me?" he asked, shock obvious in his voice.

"No, I have other plans for you. But trust me, you will remember exactly why you shouldn't disobey me when I'm done with you."

"I—I will? What are you going to do to me, sir?"

I didn't answer him. Instead, I just said, "Scoot back and keep your cock away from the edge of the bed. The only thing that can touch it is my hand."

He did as he was told, and I reached down and snapped a cuff around each of his ankles. "I'm going to attach a spreader bar to these, boy."

"Yes, sir."

"You'll enjoy being forced to stay open for me, won't you, boy?"

"Yes, Daddy."

His words were breathless, and I could hear the need in his voice. I attached the bar to the rings on each cuff. Once it was in place, he wriggled, testing his limits. "I've never had anyone use a spreader bar on me."

"Do you like how it feels?"

He nodded.

"Good. I'm going to stretch your ass now while I get you off."

"You're really going to let me come, Daddy?"

"I am." I spread lube on my fingers and wrapped a hand around his cock so I could jerk him off. He thrust his hips, pushing his shaft into the circle of my fingers as I teased his hole with my other hand, running a slickened finger around the rim, but not pushing in yet.

"Please, Daddy. Fill my hole."

I slapped his ass hard, and he jerked and cried out. "I'll fill you when I'm ready, boy, and you'll take what I give without complaint."

"Yes, sir."

"That's better." I kept working him as I teased his ass, and he flexed his hips, squirming, obviously trying to move his legs.

"You want more, boy?"

"Yes, Daddy, please don't stop."

"I'm not going to stop. I'm going to keep on and on until I've exhausted you." I pushed a finger into him then, working it slowly in and out as I continued to work his cock in firm strokes. "Are you close?"

"I'm so close. I've been wanting you all day."

"You've missed me this week, haven't you, boy?"

"Yes, Daddy. I should've called you. I should've begged you for what I needed."

"That's right, boy, but I want you to come for me now."

Sean cried out, jerking his hips and wildly thrusting into my hand. I added a second finger to his ass and worked him through his orgasm. I didn't stop touching his cock, not even when it went soft or when he started to whimper.

He sagged against the mattress, panting, and I drove my fingers in deep and pressed against his sweet spot. He cried out, sounding like he was in pain. "Daddy, please. I can't take more."

"You can, because it's what I want, and you want to be good for me."

"Yes. Good for you. I want to be a good boy." I worked a third finger into his ass and fucked him with them as I continued to stroke his cock. Eventually, he grew hard again.

"You're going to come again for me, aren't you, boy?"

"Daddy, I don't know if I can."

I slapped his ass, and he writhed, trying to get away from my hand. I spanked him again, harder. "Be still and take what I give you."

"Yes, Daddy," he sobbed.

"This is your punishment for denying us all the orgasms we could've had together while you refused to accept what you needed."

"I'm sorry, Daddy." Tears were running down his face now. I knew I was pushing him hard, but I wanted him to know this was how it would be, me giving him exactly what he needed.

"Daddy, I… I'm going to come again."

"Good, boy. Give me what I want."

He whimpered. "It's going to hurt."

"I know, boy, but this is your punishment. And when it's all over, I'm going to fuck you."

"Yes, please."

"I have to get you good and ready first." I added my pinky and pushed in deep with all four fingers, dragging over his prostate. He jerked and cried out, coming again, his cock now so slick it was hard to keep up my rhythm, but I kept going, never giving him a break as he sobbed through his orgasm.

When his body calmed, I pulled my fingers from his ass. "I'm going to get the tail plug and put it inside you. Then you're going to come for me one more time."

He whined, but didn't say anything.

I slicked up the plug, and it went in easily since he was open and ready. I flicked the tail with my hand, making it swish from side to side so he could feel it against his thighs. He groaned as I squatted down to unhook the spreader bar and take the cuffs off his ankles.

"Stand up." I helped him, knowing he might be unsteady. "Can you stay on your feet for me?"

"I think so, Daddy, but I'm kind of shaky."

"I'll keep a hold of you." I gripped his hips tight as I knelt in front of him.

"What are you doing?"

I didn't answer. I just took his cock in my mouth. It was still soft, but I knew I could get him hard again. Between the feel of the tail swishing against his legs and the feel of my throat closing around his cock, he'd get hard again. So I took my time, sucking and licking and taking him all the way down.

"Feels so good. But it hurts. It's so confusing. I just…"

He was hard now and I could taste precum leaking from the tip. I pulled off for a second and worked him with my hand. "Are you going to come again, boy?"

"Too sore. Can't."

"You're wrong, boy. I'm going to take you down my throat, and you're going to give me your cum."

"Yes, Daddy."

"If you do this for me, you'll get my cock in your ass, right beside that plug."

His eyes went wide. "You're really going to do that, Daddy?"

"Yes, boy. I'm going to fill that ass more full than it's ever been."

I took his cock back in my mouth, swallowing all of him as I worked a finger into him next to the plug. His ass was so tight, but I was determined to get my cock in there with the plug. I worked my finger in and out, and he bucked against me. I let him fuck my face until another orgasm rolled over him, and I swallowed every drop he had left to give.

I rose to my feet and kissed him, letting him taste his cum in my mouth. Then I guided him to the mirrored closet door and helped him lower himself to all fours. This time, I'd remembered to spread a towel over the carpet.

"I want you to watch me fuck you while you wear the tail. I want you to see my cock going into you, stretching you wide."

"Please," he whined.

"Do you remember your safeword?"

"It's licorice, Daddy."

"That's good, boy. Use it if you need to. I never want to force you to do anything that's too much for you."

"I want this, Daddy. I love how the tail feels in me, but I need more."

I ran my hand down his spine and over the curve of his ass. "You're Daddy's little slut, aren't you? You want your ass filled up. You want me to give you everything."

"Yes. Please."

I slicked up my cock and poured more lube around the edge of the dildo. I worked it in and out a few times and then pulled it almost all the way out and lined up my cock next to it. "Are you ready, boy?"

"So ready."

"I know it will hurt at first, but I think you're going to love it once you adjust."

"I will. I know I will."

"Look at the mirror. I want you to see." He did, and I pushed in. He tensed as soon as the tip of my cock stretched him. "It's okay. Just breathe and relax."

"It burns so bad."

His ass was squeezing me too tightly against the dildo, but the sight of us in the mirror was almost enough to make me come before we ever got started. I laid a hand on his back. "Breathe."

He panted. "Can't. Too much."

"It's okay. You can do this. Inhale." I felt his back rise.

"Good boy. Now exhale." His breath whooshed out. "Much better. Now do it again. Inhale." I paused. "Exhale. Good. Are you ready for more?"

"Yes, Daddy. Thank you."

I pushed in a little more. He whimpered, but I could feel him starting to relax. "You're doing so good, boy. I'm so proud of you. Let me in a little more."

Sean arched his spine, pushing back against me and taking me deeper. The movement surprised me, and I gasped.

On the next thrust, I sank in as far as I could go with the dildo there. Sean groaned and arched even more. "Fuck, Daddy. Please."

I could only make shallow strokes. Sean pushed back, meeting every one, like he wanted more. "That's it, boy. You're doing so good. You're going to come again, aren't you?"

"There's no way. Can't have anything left."

"I'm filling you up. I'm going to come deep inside you. Make you mine."

"Yes, please. Want to be yours."

"That's right. I know what you need." I pulled back, letting the tail slide all the way out. I dropped it to the towel and then I surged back in, going balls deep in one stroke.

"Yes!" he cried. "Need this, need you."

"Look in the mirror, boy. Watch as I own you." I reached under him to jerk him off. His cock had to be incredibly sore from all I'd demanded of him, but I wanted to make him come one last time.

I drove into him over and over as I worked him. He started to cry, but he didn't look away from our image in the mirror.

"You can do this. You can come one more time."

"I want to, Daddy. I want to be the kind of boy you want."

"Baby, you are the boy I want. No matter what you do, no matter whether you come or not, or whether you disobey, you're mine, and I love you."

"Love you. I… Fuck!" He came then, driving into my hand. His body was writhing with pain and pleasure. His ass squeezed my cock, and that was all I needed. I let go, bucking against him as I came.

We collapsed to the floor. My cock slid from his ass as I softened, but neither of us moved. We lay there, panting, covered in sweat and cum. It was absolutely perfect.

Later, when we'd cleaned up and I'd gotten Sean some water and something to eat, I held him, cuddled on my lap on the couch.

"I'm so glad you're here," I said as I ran a hand over his hair.

He lifted his head from my shoulder. His eyes were bright and filled with joy. "I love you, Blake. Thank you for being patient with me and for knowing what I needed."

"I won't always know. Sometimes you'll have to tell me or ask for what you need."

"I know, but I think I can do that now, because you'll take care of me, and it's okay for me to need that."

"It is, boy. It is completely okay."

He sucked on his lower lip for a moment, and then said, "You're really sure you want me to move in here?"

"Yes. You're my boy, and this is where you belong. I'm going to take care of you every single day."

"Mmm. I can't think of anything I want more. I'm so glad I found you."

"I'm glad you did too." I kissed him softly. He wrapped his arms around my neck, and he felt like heaven. He felt like home.

THANK YOU

Dear Reader,

Thank you for purchasing *Demanding Discipline*. I hope you enjoyed it. If you haven't read the rest of the Love and Care series, it starts with *Father of the Groom* and continues with *After the Weekend.* If you like May/December romance you may also enjoy the *Thorne and Dash* series which starts with *Professional Distance.* I offer a free book to anyone who joins my mailing list. To learn more, go to silviaviolet.com/newsletter.

Please consider leaving a review where you purchased this ebook or on Goodreads. Reviews and word-of-mouth recommendations are vital to independent authors.

I love hearing from readers. You can chat with me on Facebook in Silvia's Salon, and you can email me at silviaviolet@gmail.com. To read excerpts from all of my titles, visit my website: silviaviolet.com/books.

Silvia Violet

ABOUT THE AUTHOR

Silvia Violet writes fun, sexy stories that will leave you smiling and satisfied. She has a thing for characters who are in need of comfort and enjoys helping them surrender to love even when they doubt it exists. Silvia's stories include sizzling contemporaries, paranormals, and historicals. When she needs a break from listening to the voices in her head, she spends time baking, taking long walks, curling up with her favorite books, and spending time with her family.

Website: silviaviolet.com
Facebook: facebook.com/silvia.violet
Facebook Group: Silvia's Salon
Twitter: @Silvia_Violet
Instagram: @silvia.violet
Pinterest: pinterest.com/silviaviolet/

Thorne and Dash

Professional Distance

Personal Entanglement

Perfect Alignment

Well-Tailored (A Thorne and Dash Companion Story)

Ames Bridge

Down on the Farm

The Past Comes Home

Tied to Home

Unexpected

Unexpected Rescue

Unexpected Trust

Unexpected Engagement

Law and Supernatural Order

Sex on the Hoof

Paws on Me

Dinner at Foxy's

Hoofing' It To The Altar

Wild R Farm

Finding Release

Arresting Love

Embracing Need

Taming Tristan

Willing Hands

Shifting Hearts

Wild R Christmas

Printed in Poland
by Amazon Fulfillment
Poland Sp. z o.o., Wrocław

36241833R00101